Life. Is. Not. Fair.

Also by Gary W. Bargar

What Happened to Mr. Forster?

· Gary W. Bargar ·

Life. Is. Not. Fair.

Clarion Books

TICKNOR & FIELDS: A HOUGHTON MIFFLIN COMPANY

New York

The author is grateful to J. Fred Coots, composer, for permission to quote from "Santa Claus Is Coming to Town" by J. Fred Coots and Haven Gillespie, published by Leo Feist, Inc. and to Chappell and Company for lyrics from "I'm Beginning to See the Light" by Duke Ellington, Don George, Johnny Hodges, and Harry James, © 1944 by Alamo Music, Inc., copyright renewed, assigned to Chappell and Co., Inc. (Intersong Music, Publisher). International copyright secured. ALL RIGHTS RESERVED. Used by permission.

Finally, the author thanks Margaret Gabel and the members of her Workshop in Writing for Children at the New School for their continuing criticism, encouragement, and friendship.

Clarion Books
Ticknor & Fields, a Houghton Mifflin Company
Copyright © 1984 by Gary W. Bargar

Printed in the U.S.A.

Library of Congress Cataloging in Publication Data
Bargar, Gary W.
   Life. Is. Not. Fair.

   Summary: Louis and his aunt are startled and upset
when a black family moves next door to their Kansas City
home in 1959, but Louis soon recognizes that his new
neighbor is a more reliable friend than the group of
junior high "cools" with whom he had hoped to be friends.
   [1. Friendship—Fiction.   2. Prejudices—Fiction.
3. Race relations—Fiction.   4. Afro-Americans—Fiction.]
I. Title.
PZ7.B25037Li 1984   [Fic]   83-15299
ISBN 0-89919-218-1

s 10 9 8 7 6 5 4 3 2 1

This book is for Rusty.

· Chapter One ·

SOMETHING HAD COME over Aunt Zona.
Late in August the Tooheys, who had been our next-door neighbors for as long as I could remember, suddenly packed up and moved out. Right away Aunt Zona began to get very jittery about the house next door. Several times a day I'd find her standing at the dining room windows, her head bobbing back and forth like a parakeet's, a sharp, searching look in her eye. The empty house next door rose up blank and wide outside our windows. There was never a sign of life over there. I couldn't see what Aunt Zona was watching.

One time I asked her.

Aunt Zona gave me a doubtful look, as if she wasn't quite sure whether she wanted to give up her secret. Then she said, "Reverend Hardcastle's wife says the colored are getting ready to take over this neighborhood. Just three weeks ago a family moved in on the Hardcastles' block. The next day five For Sale signs went up. And that's only nine blocks away from here."

"I don't see what that has to do with the Tooheys," I said.

I

Aunt Zona looked exasperated. "Billy Lou, don't be so dense. We're next! Why do you think the Tooheys left so fast? Why do you think there's no For Sale sign on the lawn? They've already sold! To the colored! You mark my words. I'm just waiting to see who moves into that house."

"Call me Louis, Aunt Zona," I said mildly. For the nine hundredth time. Aunt Zona was just about the only person left who still called me Billy Lou. Now that I was about to start seventh grade, it was high time for her to get trained.

Aunt Zona's sharp look softened for a minute. "You'll always be my little Billy Lou to me," she said. I had to run to my room before she got mushy.

I didn't have too much time to worry about Aunt Zona and colored people, though. School was opening in a week, and I had lots of shopping to do. This would be my first year at Emerson Junior High. I had to start out right. On Monday I went out and bought a ninety-nine-cent loose-leaf notebook that held five hundred sheets. That same night my best friend, Paul Harte, called up and told me to take it back. "Only dips carry those around, Louis," Paul said. "You don't want people to think you're a dip."

In grade school, just about everyone except Paul had thought I was a dip. Being a dip was worse than having buck teeth. Buck teeth could be straightened, but dippiness just clung to you like some terrible invisible icing. "What should I get?" I asked Paul.

"A clipboard," Paul said. "Everyone at Emerson has a clipboard. Clipboards are very cool."

So I went back to Parkview Drugstore and bought a clipboard. The clipboard cost $1.29, but it was worth it. The opposite of a dip was a cool. Paul and I were going to become cools.

Of course, just owning a clipboard wasn't enough to make you a cool. I wrote that very sentence in my journal, to prove how realistic I was being about it all. You had to dress right, too. Paul said the worst possible thing to wear was dark socks. The day after I bought the clipboard, I went through all my drawers and threw out every pair of dark socks I could find.

When she saw what I was doing, Aunt Zona had a fit. "Billy Lou Lamb, you know what I always tell you. Waste not, want not. Think of all the starving children in India. They'd be thrilled to have those socks."

"In India it's too hot to wear socks," I said.

Aunt Zona surged ahead. "Money doesn't grow on trees, Billy Lou. If you think I'm going to spend money to buy a dozen pairs of new socks when you've got all these perfectly good ones, you've got another think coming."

Someday, I knew, I was going to be a famous writer. Mr. Forster, a teacher I'd had last year, had told me I had real talent. I'd been keeping a journal ever since. When I was at the top of the best-seller list, I'd have money for thousands of socks. All white. But I didn't tell Aunt Zona that. I just said, "I don't need a dozen pairs of new socks. I can just buy two pairs of white socks and wash the dirty pair out in the sink after school every day."

Aunt Zona snorted at me.

"Anyway," I said, "I've been saving my allowance all summer. I've got enough money to buy the socks myself. You won't have to spend a penny."

Aunt Zona left my room without saying more. That was another thing. Aunt Zona was growing hard to get along with. When I was a little kid, we'd never had fights. Now we argued about everything. Paul said his parents were the same way. "I think it's the shock of seeing us go off to junior high. We're getting away from them, and they don't like it," Paul said. "They're starting to panic."

I wasn't so sure. When I was fifty years old and bald, with my own set of false teeth, Aunt Zona would probably still be calling me her little Billy Lou and cutting up my steaks for me, just like always. Aunt Zona never seemed to notice that I was growing up, no matter how much I changed.

The day after the sock argument was the day Aunt Zona finally went completely haywire. August 26, 1959. That was the day the moving truck pulled up in front of the Toohey house.

Aunt Zona had been baking something when we heard the banging sounds of the truck doors. She was out of the kitchen in seconds. She dashed into the living room to look out the picture window, then to the dining room to peer out the side ones. "They're here! They're

4

here! What did I tell you, Billy Lou? What did I tell you?"

I tried to see over her shoulder.

"Turn on the radio, Billy Lou," Aunt Zona hollered. "Turn it to that rock and roll station you like, that WHB. Turn the sound up all the way. Then help me open up all these windows."

I just stared at her. Aunt Zona hated WHB. She hardly ever let me play that station. Aunt Zona liked Mantovani and Lawrence Welk and songs from the Broadman Hymnal. Not rock and roll.

"Don't just stand there with your mouth open. Make it snappy!" Aunt Zona was already raising windows all along the side of the house.

I went to the kitchen.

Slowly I moved toward the radio next to the breakfast table. I wondered if Aunt Zona could be having a nervous breakdown. In my sixth-grade class we'd had a first-aid course. We'd learned what to do if someone went into shock. I eyed Aunt Zona nervously, but she didn't seem to be about to pass out. I didn't know what the first aid was for a plain nervous breakdown.

I switched on the radio. Connie Francis blasted into the kitchen singing "Lipstick on Your Collar."

I walked back to the dining room, where Aunt Zona was struggling to open the windows from the top as well as the bottom. "What are we doing this for?" I asked.

"Don't you see, Billy Lou? If we make a lot of noise, maybe the colored people will think we give wild parties all the time. Maybe they won't want to move next door to us. They might just turn around and go right back where they came from." Aunt Zona began to sing along with Connie Francis. She didn't know the words and she wasn't quite on key, but she was good and loud.

I trailed her into the living room. "Aunt Zona," I said, but she didn't hear me. "AUNT ZONA!" I yelled. "This is silly. We haven't even met these people yet. They might be very nice."

"Oh, I don't have anything against *nice* colored people. We're all God's children, that's what I always say. Don't I always say that, Billy Lou? There are lots of very fine colored people, like that Mahalia Jackson we saw on Ed Sullivan. You just don't know who they might bring into the neighborhood, that's all. What are their relatives like? That's what worries me!" By the time she'd opened the last window, Aunt Zona seemed to have run out of energy. She flopped onto the sofa and stared off into space.

I started to walk out the front door.

"Billy Lou, where are you going?"

"I thought I'd go out on the front porch and watch. After all, I haven't seen what the new people look like."

Aunt Zona jumped up again. "You come right back here. We don't want them to think they got our goat. We can see everything from in here."

We went back to the dining room. Aunt Zona stood just next to the dining room curtain. I stood behind her, watching from an angle. A cream-colored Oldsmobile had pulled up behind the moving van. Two people got

6

out. Aunt Zona was right. They were both colored. There was a stiff, light-skinned woman carrying a crystal lamp. She was looking around the block, absolutely expressionless. There was also a caramel-colored boy about my own age running up to the Toohey's mailbox. He seemed to be glancing at our house as he ran.

"I don't think the music is going to make them turn around and leave," I said. "Maybe we should turn the radio off."

Aunt Zona said, "They look nice and clean, anyway. I'll say that for them."

"I wonder if the boy is in my grade. He'll probably go to Emerson."

This set Aunt Zona off again. She talked about how there had never been colored students at Emerson. In her day, Aunt Zona said, the colored in Kansas City had had their own schools, with separate books and erasers and everything. She said that if the colored boy sat next to me in class, I should just be polite and pretend he wasn't there.

While she was still going on, I went to the kitchen and turned off the radio. In the sudden silence, the knock on our front door was startlingly loud.

"Oh, my Lord, they're coming over here already," Aunt Zona said. "It's not enough just to move in. They have to start integrating right away."

I was already on my way to the living room. "I'll get it," I said, but Aunt Zona was at my heels.

I made it to the door a split second ahead of her.

The boy from next door was standing on our porch.

7

This close, the first thing I noticed about him was his eyes. They were ice blue. I never thought Negroes could have blue eyes. These were the kind of eyes that seem to look along a straight line that runs right through you, though the boy wasn't staring. He had a small, polite smile on his face. "Hi," he said.

"Hi," I said. I twisted my trouser leg, feeling awkward.

"Is there something we can do for you?" Aunt Zona said.

"Yes, ma'am. I'm DeWitt Clauson. My family is moving in next door. You probably noticed our truck. The Tooheys were supposed to leave the house keys in the mailbox, but they're not in there. We can't get into the house. We wondered if they might have given the keys to you."

"No, I'm afraid they didn't," Aunt Zona said. "We don't know anything about any keys."

"Oh," DeWitt Clauson said. "Well, do you think I might use your telephone to call Mrs. Toohey?"

I started to open the screen door to let him in, but I felt a kick on the back of my leg. Aunt Zona said, "I'm sorry, but our phone is out of order. I don't know when it'll be fixed."

I felt my stomach lurch, as if something had hit it. I'd never heard Aunt Zona tell a lie before. Not ever. I couldn't face DeWitt Clauson. I had to look away.

When I looked again, he was already backing up toward the porch steps. DeWitt's face had a frozen look. "I see," he was saying. "Thank you just the same."

8

Then he was running down the steps and across the lawn.

I turned to Aunt Zona.

Aunt Zona flushed. "It was just a little fib," she said weakly.

In its nook in the dining room, our phone started to ring. With all the windows open, the rings would carry out onto our lawn, over to the spot on the walk next door where the Clausons were still standing. With all our windows open, they would hear every single ring.

·Chapter Two·

ON THE FIRST day of school it took me two hours to dress. The only thing I was sure about was my socks. I had put on one of the new white pairs I'd just bought. At least my ankles would look like a cool's. The rest of my outfit gave me trouble. There was my shirt. Aunt Zona wanted me to wear a freshly starched white shirt and a clip-on tie, but I put my foot down. I might as well paint the word *dip* on my forehead. No, it was between a plaid flannel shirt and a plain yellow one. I tried on both shirts about five times each and finally settled on the yellow.

Some wheat-colored chinos went nicely with the yellow shirt, but I got stuck again on the shoes. At first I put on sneakers, but Aunt Zona wouldn't let me out of the house in those, so I had to go back and change into some slightly scuffed-up penny loafers. Just so they didn't look too new. Cool was sloppy. Only dips wore new clothes that *looked* new.

I grabbed my clipboard off the bench in my bedroom and gave myself one long last look in the full-length mirror on the closet door.

Aunt Zona came up behind me. "Better put something on your head, Billy Lou. It's chilly out this morning." She held out a moth-eaten Kansas City A's baseball cap I'd almost outgrown.

"I'm fine, Aunt Zona," I said, heading for the living room. I had to take giant steps to stay out of Aunt Zona's reach. The last thing I needed was some dippy baseball cap on my head. It would spoil the whole effect.

I made it to the front door, and the screen closed practically in Aunt Zona's face. I was down the porch steps before she could get her momentum back.

Emerson Junior High was a longer walk from our house than my grade school had been — over a mile. I came up to the school from behind, so I didn't get the full effect until I rounded the corner of Emerson Parkway. I'd seen the building before, of course, on Orientation Day last spring, but I couldn't help being impressed all over again. Emerson Junior High had been built about thirty years ago, and the architect had been crazy for castles. The building was enormous, with turrets rising from either end and a magnificent stone belfry in the middle.

The lawn was huge, too, but what really set the campus off was the forest on the other side of it. That is, it reminded me of a forest — maybe Sherwood. Actually it was a park, Emerson Park, the biggest park in the city, in the whole state. At the entrance, an arch surrounded by close-trimmed shrubs opened onto a long, tree-lined passage that looked silent and deserted, even with nine hundred noisy kids milling around a few hundred feet away. The whole park seemed to breathe at you. Patiently.

A hand came down on my shoulder. I jumped.

"You made it," Paul said.

"Oh, hi." I forced myself to exhale slowly. If I was going to be a cool, I couldn't be the nervous type.

"Notice the sweater," Paul said. He was wearing a midnight-blue cardigan with white trim. "Emerson colors! I borrowed it from my neighbor. You ought to get one."

"Do I look okay?" Somehow everything Paul said made me more nervous.

"You look like a giant lemon with legs. What made you wear that yellow shirt?"

"Aunt Zona forced me," I lied. I exhaled again and made a mental note to involve my shirt in a fatal accident when I got home this afternoon. Just then a bell shrilled inside the school building.

A voice blared from a speaker somewhere in the belfry. "Attention, all students. Proceed to the auditorium for induction assembly."

Everyone herded toward the oak front doors.

I stuck close to Paul. With all these kids pushing and cramming around us, I didn't want to lose him. The only friend I had in all this crowd.

You almost didn't have to put your feet down. The tide carried you along. Through the open doors, across a rotunda with a polished marble floor, into the school auditorium. An auditorium twice as big as the one at Louisa May Alcott, my grade school.

Paul and I found seats near the back. Paul punched me. "There's Veronica Allison," he hissed. That was a girl from our grade school. Sure enough, Veronica was sitting across the aisle and a few rows down. She was wearing her hair in a bun on top of her head. Veronica had lost weight and grown much taller over the summer. She didn't look chubby anymore. With the bun she looked approximately thirty years old.

I started to make a crack to Paul, but someone said, "Excuse me," and pushed in front of us on her way toward an empty seat down the row. There was something familiar about the girl. She was very skinny, but her midnight-blue and white pullover sweater showed an unusually large bust. A charm bracelet clinked on each wrist, and her glistening fingernails were at least two inches long. The girl had plastered on several layers of lipstick and rouge, but I felt sure I knew the face underneath. Then it hit me.

"Paul," I whispered. "That's Ellie. Ellie Siegel."

Paul's head snapped to the left for a better look. "Good Lord," he said. "It *is*. Look at the size of her chest! It can't be real! How could anyone grow so much over one summer? Especially Ellie."

Ellie Siegel had been the biggest dip in our grade school. Much worse than I'd ever been. She sure looked different now.

"She looks like an ad for that movie *High School Confidential*," Paul said.

"Aunt Zona won't let me see that," I said. There were lots of movies Aunt Zona wouldn't let me see. For example, anything with Ingrid Bergman in it. Aunt Zona said that Ingrid Bergman was a hussy, ever since she left her husband to run off with an Italian.

On stage a tall, white-haired man had come up to the podium. He tapped on the microphone a few times. The sound system crackled. I recognized the man from Orientation. He was Elgin D. Reilly, the principal. "Greetings, students," Mr. Reilly said into the microphone. It squealed deafeningly. A custodian in a gray uniform trotted onto the stage and began fiddling with it.

Mr. Reilly began again. By now the room was getting quiet. "Welcome to the Guild Hall." I knew that the Guild Hall was Emerson. Emerson Junior High had a medieval theme. Seventh-graders were called Apprentices, eighth-graders Journeymen, and ninth-graders Masters. The athletic teams were all called Jousters. Mr. Reilly explained all this again. "There will be many a tournament for you to face in the coming year," he said. "I refer not only to those tournaments on the field of combat — "

"He means football," Paul told me.

" — but to those rigorous trials by fire and water in the classroom. I know that our fine students will be more than equal to these tests, that you will sally forth bravely to slay your dragons with banners flying high."

Someone a couple of rows ahead of us made a loud raspberry.

Mr. Reilly ignored it. "And in conclusion, as we begin another new term, I challenge you with this thought:

"Wear proudly your colors of pristine white
and midnight blue!
Always join the construction gang, and never
the wrecking crew."

From somewhere offstage a piano sounded an opening chord. Everyone stood up. Some of the kids were starting to sing. I recognized the school song, but I didn't know the words, so I just hummed along. Mr. Reilly stood at attention by the microphone until the song was over. Then a woman walked on stage, a sheaf of papers in her hand.

She turned out to be one of the guidance counselors. She told us where to go to pick up our class schedule cards. There were tables set up in the first-floor halls. You went to the table that had the cards for the first letter of your last name.

Before the woman had even finished speaking, kids were heading for the auditorium doors. The woman stamped her foot and fluttered her papers, but that only made more kids get up. Pretty soon the noise of shuffling feet drowned her out completely, so Paul and I got up, too.

Just before we separated in the hall to pick up our schedules, my hands began to get sweaty, and I felt an invisible fist clench in my stomach. My shirt seemed yellower than ever, and there was no way to hide it. I knew I must be getting B.O. I wanted to test my arm-pits, but I couldn't do that here. Someone would be sure to notice. The only good things about me were my socks and my clipboard. And it struck me suddenly that nobody was going to see my socks. I didn't want to leave Paul. What if we didn't have any classes together?

But all I said was, "See you later — "

"Alligator," Paul finished. And was gone down the hall before I could think of anything else to add.

I turned the other way and headed for the *L* table.

A voice from nowhere shouted, "Howdy, Lulu-belle!"

Automatically, I looked around. Then I bit into my tongue. The very worst thing to do. I knew right away who was calling. Mickey Blake, another kid from Al-cott. Mickey was slouched against a locker in the mid-dle of a group of guys I didn't recognize. Every one of them had an oily ducktail haircut, including Mickey. Hoods. J.D.'s. Greasers.

Mickey blew me a kiss. "Good to see ya, babe. Come on over and meet my friends."

I shook my head and kept going, stiff-lipped. Mickey had been riding me for months. In grade school, I'd got-ten used to Mickey Blake. Could even ignore him most of the time. Today Mickey seemed downright dan-gerous.

"Bye-bye, LOOO-lubelle." A whole chorus of mock-ing voices followed me down the hall.

I tried to make my face look completely blank. If I didn't turn around again, most of the kids wouldn't know who those guys were talking to. Lulubelle could be anyone.

Halfway down the hall I found the right table and picked up my card. I glanced quickly over it: the usual classes. Math, Language Arts, Social Studies, Physical Education, Speech, and first-year Spanish. Phys Ed was first. I groaned. My very worst, my least favorite subject, and it had to come first.

Oh, well. Nothing I could do about that.

From the Orientation tour, I dimly remembered that the gym was in the east wing. The opposite direction. I would have to backtrack, right past Mickey Blake and his hoody friends. My whole body prickled with perspiration.

I wiped my palms on my chinos and straightened my back. I'd just walk fast, keeping my face like stone.

But when I got to the spot where Mickey's gang had been standing, they weren't there anymore. I let out a deep breath. I could relax.

The metal part of my clipboard had been cutting into my right hand. I flexed my fingers. Now I was strolling, just strolling, all the way down the east corridor. Nobody could take me for a dip.

Pretty soon a dank, raunchy smell reached my nostrils, and I knew I was almost at the gym area. I rounded a corner, and the marble part of the floor gave way to plain charcoal-colored concrete.

I saw them right away, lounging at the big double door to the gym, blocking the threshold. Mickey Blake and two of his friends, chomping on their gum and grinning, but not at me, at the person walking just a few feet ahead of me.

There was no mistaking DeWitt Clauson, even from the back. DeWitt was wearing a fresh white shirt, exactly the kind Aunt Zona had tried to make me put on this morning. Maybe his mother had argued louder than Aunt Zona, or maybe DeWitt Clauson just didn't know that you didn't wear a white shirt to this school. Worse still, he was carrying a fat loose-leaf notebook — with dividers, yet. I was walking faster than DeWitt. In a few seconds I'd overtake him. Something made me slow down.

It was partly that I was still embarrassed by the way Aunt Zona had acted the other day and I didn't want to have to talk to DeWitt. Also, I didn't like the way Mickey and his friends were looking at DeWitt, and I didn't know what to do about it.

I waited for them to start making catcalls, or dirty jokes, but the hall was completely quiet, except for the sounds of two pairs of feet. Mine and DeWitt's. My own steps got slower and slower. It was as if the concrete floor were a giant magnet, and my shoes had iron soles.

I had to admire DeWitt Clauson. He didn't miss a beat, just kept on going, didn't even flinch. When he got to the doorway, he started to say "Pardon me" in a clear, crisp voice.

He never got it out. Mickey's leg came up, his friends shoved DeWitt from behind, and DeWitt crashed headlong onto the gymnasium floor. His notebook flew open. Blank papers rippled across the floorboards.

I started to step forward, but there was a commotion inside the gym. Several other kids gathered around De-Witt, then a gray-haired man with a whistle around his neck pushed through them.

"What's going on here?"

DeWitt stirred, picked himself up, and began to brush his slacks off in a dazed way.

Mickey and his friends sauntered on across the threshold. The man with the whistle stopped them. "I asked a question," he said.

"Nothing happened, Mr. Sharp," one of Mickey's friends said smoothly. "This kid in front of us just tripped, that's all."

"Is that right?" Mr. Sharp asked DeWitt.

DeWitt kept brushing himself. He didn't speak.

Mr. Sharp glanced at me. "You see anything?"

I swallowed. "I —"

They were all looking at me now. Mr. Sharp, DeWitt Clauson, Mickey Blake, Mickey's friends. Over their shoulders I could see that one of the other guys in the gym was Paul. I sent him a look, hoping somehow Paul could get me out of this. But Paul's face wore a neutral expression.

I swallowed again. Finally I said, "N-no. I didn't see anything."

DeWitt's ice-blue stare thrust forward along its invisible track, met my eyes, passed through, and then seemed just to shut itself off. DeWitt turned and started to pick up his notebook and his papers.

I walked past him into the gym. My legs felt shaky.

"Thanks, Lulubelle," Mickey said, loud enough for everyone around us to hear.

I walked on, found Paul, and sat down with him on the wooden floor. I glanced sideways. Was Paul embarrassed for me? Did he think I'd done the right thing? Paul looked straight ahead while Mr. Sharp got ready to call the roll. I couldn't tell what he was thinking.

But it didn't really matter. I knew the truth. A piece of DeWitt Clauson's ice-blue stare had chipped off and stuck inside me, and whichever way I moved, it hurt.

· Chapter Three ·

S TOP STEWING about it, Louis," Paul said as we
walked down Fifty-ninth Street that afternoon. It's
not such a big deal."

"I *lied!* I'm as bad as Aunt Zona. Worse! DeWitt
could have gotten really hurt." I slapped my clipboard
hard against my thigh, hoping to bruise myself.

"So could you," Paul said. "Those thugs would have
mashed you to jelly after school if you'd told on them.
You know they would."

"Boy, Mickey Blake was never that bad in grade
school. To think he could have gotten so low in just one
summer."

"Blake's a degenerate," Paul said, but he didn't sound
particularly disgusted.

"Maybe I should go over to DeWitt's house and talk
to him," I said. "That is, if he'd even listen to me."

"I think you should just let it go. You don't want to
get mixed up with that guy. He's going to have lots of
problems at Emerson, and the farther you stay away
from him, the better it'll be for you."

I stared. This didn't sound like Paul. Paul was usually
so understanding. "But—"

"Here's where I turn off. See you tomorrow!" Paul left me with a bare offhand wave.

I muttered some kind of good-bye and walked on. I tried to think about the other things that had happened today. About my new teachers, for instance. Six of them! That was a lot to digest. In grade school, you got used to the same old face at the teacher's desk every day. Within two weeks you knew every routine the teacher had. The whole second semester of sixth grade, the only time I'd ever had to listen to the teacher was during spelling tests. And I'd gotten all *highs* on my report card. Now it would be different.

But I couldn't get my mind off DeWitt Clauson. The look he'd given me in the gym. I shivered. How could one look make me feel so . . . *guilty?* Not the right word. *Responsible*, maybe. But I couldn't be responsible for DeWitt Clauson. I scarcely knew the guy.

By the time I reached my own block, I found myself walking all hunched over, like a crook in an old Peter Lorre movie. As I turned onto our walk, I glanced at the Clausons' house. Nothing moved over there. De-Witt probably wasn't exactly watching for me. I could sneak right by. Unless I decided to cross the lawn. Unless I decided to go over there and ring the doorbell and talk to DeWitt and say — what? *I'm sorry?*

I couldn't do it. I was on the porch and into our living room before I could even finish the thought.

"Aunt Zona?"

She didn't answer.

"Hello?" I shouted. Aunt Zona usually met me at the door, half the time with a cupcake and a glass of milk. Here she was acting strange again, and just when I didn't need one more thing to worry about. "Anybody home?"

"Oh, Billy Lou! In here!" Aunt Zona's muffled voice came from the spare bedroom, the one that used to be the den when Uncle Emmett was still alive.

I wasn't expecting the sight that greeted me when I got back there. Aunt Zona was just crawling backwards out of the closet, one hand full of different colored bills and canceled checks. The rug and all the chairs were littered with folded-up pieces of paper, some of which looked old and tattered. I glanced at the writing on one yellowish bundle by my shoe. Most of the print was too small to read, but I could tell that it was an insurance policy of some kind. "Aunt Zona? What are you doing?"

Aunt Zona set her handful of papers down in a clear space on the rug. Then she made me help her to her feet. "You got home just in time, Billy Lou," she said. "If you hadn't been here I might have had to stay on my hands and knees all night. These old joints don't bend like they used to."

"What is all this?" I kicked at some of the papers.

"Well, I guess you might say I've been going over our finances. What with one thing and another, I figure we might need some extra cash soon."

"What for, Aunt Zona?"

"Don't get your dirty footprints on my will, Billy Lou."

I moved my foot. "Why do we need extra cash?"

Aunt Zona's forehead puckered. "First off, there's your college education. We only have six more years to save up for that, and our little nest egg will only go so far." She paused and looked across at me from under lowered eyebrows. "And there's the house. What with colored people moving in under our noses right and left, we might have to sell any day now. Then we'd need a down payment on a new house."

I cleared a chair of folded-up papers and sat down, blinking at Aunt Zona.

"Now, I don't want you to worry about anything," she said. "Not for one minute. It's all in the Lord's hands. You know how I always tell you the Lord is watching over us?"

I nodded.

"Well, he's already given me an idea. Billy Lou, pretty soon we'll have as much extra cash as we need."

"What kind of idea?"

"Well, sir, just Sunday night I was sitting here at home watching *What's My Line*, same as usual, when this kid comes on, barely twenty years old, and it turns out he's the president of a bubblegum company. A millionaire! Even that Dorothy Kilgallen couldn't guess his line, and you know how smart she is. That's when my little voice spoke. It said, 'Zona May Crenshaw, you could do that'."

"I don't get it," I said crossly. "You're going to make bubblegum?" Something about all this was bothering me. I wasn't sure yet what.

"Make bubblegum! What an idea! No! But you know how Uncle Emmett and I ran the store all those years?"

I nodded again. Aunt Zona and Uncle Emmett had owned a confectionery parlor in Armourdale, Kansas, during the Depression. They'd sold candy and pies and ice-cream sodas and stuff.

"Well, my little voice said to me, 'Zona May Crenshaw, go back to what you do best and earn your fortune.' One thing all our customers used to say was how good my divinity was. Why, we used to get bums off the street who hardly had a dime for a cup of coffee, and would they ask us for money? No, they'd ask for a piece of my good divinity. 'Zona May Crenshaw,' my voice said, 'you may not have the store anymore, but you can still make divinity. You just start your own divinity company and the world will beat a path to your door.'"

"But how do you know the world will beat a path to your door?" I said. "I don't know anyone who eats divinity nowadays." I tried to remember the last time Aunt Zona had made the white, sweet, sticky stuff. I'd rather eat fudge.

"It's all part of the Lord's plan," Aunt Zona said serenely. "This is how he's going to get you to college and me into a decent neighborhood for my old age.

With the profits from my divinity. You just wait and see."

"Aunt Zona, I don't see how you can be so sure—"

"You wait and see," she repeated. Aunt Zona waved her hand with a flourish to dismiss the subject, then she went on into the kitchen to get my cupcake.

I just kept sitting there, frowning. Sometimes it was impossible to talk sense to Aunt Zona. Especially when her little voice started speaking to her. That same little voice had told her to buy the confectionery store in Armourdale and to ditch her first boyfriend, Mr. MacIlhenny, and marry Uncle Emmett. Aunt Zona's little voice had a good track record, I had to admit. But this time I was suspicious of it.

How did Aunt Zona know that God's plan was for her to sell divinity? She always seemed so positive about things like that. I prayed all the time, too, just like Aunt Zona, but so far, the Lord had never said anything to me. Not a word. Every time I tried to picture him, all I could come up with was a kind of white, rolling mist that you couldn't see through, pouring over an endless sky. I wasn't really sure I wanted to know what was behind the white mist. I might be struck dead or something.

I knew one thing from experience. When anything was bothering me, the best cure was to take out my journal and write about it. Today I had two problems to write about. DeWitt Clauson and Aunt Zona's little voice.

"Billy Lou? Come and get it!" Aunt Zona called from the kitchen.

"No, thanks, Aunt Zona," I called back. "I'm not hungry. I'll be in my room if you want me."

I went to find my journal.

*

I was able to put Aunt Zona's little voice out of my mind for a while, but I couldn't quite shake DeWitt Clauson. I saw DeWitt every day. He was in two of my classes besides gym: Language Arts and Spanish. We never spoke to each other. We hardly even glanced at each other. I was still sort of ashamed of myself. And DeWitt, if he thought anything at all about me, must have decided I was no better than Mickey Blake and his friends.

One morning DeWitt Clauson turned up where I least expected him. In my Sunday School class at the New Jerusalem Baptist Church.

I walked through the door of the Chi Rho room — that was the seventh- and eighth-grade class — to find DeWitt sitting right smack in the middle of the semicircle of chairs. He was wearing a sharp, new-looking navy blue suit, nicer than my old gray one, which was getting too short at the wrists. DeWitt's Bible looked fancier than mine, too. Some of the kids nearby, like Veronica Allison and Claudia Hardcastle, were giving him curious looks out of the corners of their eyes.

Claudia's father was our pastor, and her mother

taught the Chi Rho class. Mrs. Hardcastle had moved up from the sixth-grade class, the Young Galileans, which she'd taught last year. She told us she'd been "promoted" and laughed as if she'd cracked a hilarious joke. Personally, I thought she was just following Claudia around so she could keep an eye on her.

Today Mrs. Hardcastle was very busy thumbing through her Bible and not looking at DeWitt Clauson. Her face was pink, and her silver-blue wig looked a little off center, as it usually did when she got worked up about something.

I guessed Mrs. Hardcastle, like everybody else, was wondering why DeWitt was here, why the Clausons had decided to come to our church. I wondered, too.

The only empty seats were on either side of DeWitt. I sat down on his left, not sure whether I should say something or not. Before I could get a "Hi" out, the buzzer rang to start class.

Mrs. Hardcastle took a breath. "Girls and boys, as you can see, we have a visitor this morning. This is De-Witt Clauson, who belongs at Mount Sinai Baptist, down around Fifteenth and Paseo. We're just real glad to have you today, DeWitt." It seemed to me that Mrs. Hardcastle bore down on the *today*. She flashed an airy smile toward DeWitt without actually looking straight at him.

DeWitt gave a nod and a tiny twitch of a smile back.

Mrs. Hardcastle moved on to the Memory Verses. Each week you were supposed to memorize a passage from the Bible that was printed in the Sunday School quarterly. Mrs. Hardcastle was a stickler. She made every single person say the verse in front of the whole class. If you got it right, she put a star by your name in the roll book. I was all set. This week's verse was easy: *For I know that my redeemer liveth, and that he shall stand at the latter day upon the earth.* Job 19:25. We'd been studying Job for the last two weeks.

Mrs. Hardcastle began with the seats nearest the window, grilling people and licking stars. When she got to DeWitt, she beamed another of her vague smiles at his vicinity and said, "Since you're just visiting, DeWitt, you may recite any Bible verse you care to. They do memorize Bible verses at your church, don't they?"

"Oh, yes, ma'am," DeWitt said. He shifted in his chair. I wondered if he felt nervous.

"Well, go right ahead, then." Mrs. Hardcastle clasped her hands behind her roll book.

DeWitt began: *"Many waters cannot quench love, neither can the floods drown it: if a man would give all the substance of his house for love, it would utterly be contemned.* Song of Solomon 8:7." When DeWitt recited, his voice sounded strong and rich and confident. It was the voice of someone who was used to performing in front of people.

Mrs. Hardcastle let out a surprised, "Oh. Why, that was beautiful, DeWitt." Her eyes focused in on him for the first time, as if he were an old friend she'd just picked out of a crowd in a bus station. "You have a wonderful speaking voice. Please go on."

DeWitt might have smiled. I couldn't see. But he

29

continued: *"We have a little sister, and she hath no breasts: what shall we do for our sister in the day when she shall be sp—"*

Guffaws erupted from the part of the room where most of the boys were sitting.

"That will do." Mrs. Hardcastle set her roll book and stars on the table and folded her arms. She raked the boys with a look. "I know what you're laughing at," she said, "and it *isn't* funny." Her glare grazed DeWitt briefly.

Then she had us all open our quarterlies. We never did finish the Memory Verses.

I'd been trying to keep a grin hidden behind my hand. I sneaked a sidelong look at DeWitt. His face was sober. You couldn't tell if he'd chosen those verses on purpose or not, but I had a hunch he knew exactly what he was doing. Sunday School was certainly a lot less boring with DeWitt in it. I couldn't wait to see if he'd say anything else.

Mrs. Hardcastle was reviewing the part of Job we'd already covered. The part where Satan bets God that he can make Job curse God to his face, and God lets Satan do all these terrible things to make Job suffer. It's kind of grisly. Job loses his animals, his children all die, and then he gets covered with boils from the soles of his feet to the crown of his head.

"You'd be miserable, too, if you were covered with boils," Mrs. Hardcastle said. I wondered if she was talking from personal experience.

Job gets very depressed by everything that happens,

but he doesn't curse God. After that, a bunch of friends come along to try to comfort him, but all except Elihu, the youngest, seem to think Job is being punished because he's sinned. They say that God rewards the virtuous and punishes the guilty. Job keeps saying that he's innocent, that there's no reason for him to be suffering.

Finally God himself comes along in a whirlwind and answers Job. That's the part we were studying today.

Mrs. Hardcastle had Veronica begin the section where God's voice comes out of the whirlwind. Veronica liked to tell people she was going to become an actress when she grew up, so she read the verses very dramatically. She still wasn't even close to my idea of what God would sound like.

Veronica read:

"Where wast thou when I laid the foundations of the earth? declare, if thou hast understanding. Who hath laid the measures thereof, if thou knowest? or who hath stretched the line upon it? Whereupon are the foundations thereof fastened? or who laid the corner stone thereof; When the morning stars sang together, and all the sons of God shouted for joy?"

We talked about what God was saying to Job. Mrs. Hardcastle said the Lord was telling us that he's God and we're not and so we have no right to question his will, no matter how much we suffer.

DeWitt gave a muffled grunt.

Mrs. Hardcastle cast her eyes toward heaven. "Did you have something to add, DeWitt?" she asked coldly.

DeWitt said, "Well, no, not exactly, Mrs. Hardcastle.

31

I was just wondering why God would bother to make the whirlwind and talk to Job if he thought Job had no right to question his will. I mean, why would he pay any attention to Job at all?"

Mrs. Hardcastle looked dumbfounded.

"Especially," DeWitt went on, "since it was God who let Satan do all those awful things to Job. Didn't Job have a right to complain about that?"

"And anyway," Veronica put in, "stars can't sing."

We heard Mrs. Hardcastle take in a few breaths. She muttered something about "questioning your Maker." Then she said firmly, "Willa Jean Marshall, read the next five verses, please," and the class rolled on.

I wanted Mrs. Hardcastle to answer DeWitt's questions, but you could tell she never would. That DeWitt. I'd never met anyone so brave.

*

For the rest of the class period, DeWitt Clauson sat quietly in his chair, following along while other people read passages from Job. Mrs. Hardcastle managed not to call on him again at all.

When the buzzer sounded for class to end, DeWitt walked out of the room by himself, ahead of everybody else. Most of the kids were forming groups either to sit together in the sanctuary or to walk home together. I thought now might be a good time for me to say something to DeWitt, so I set off at a brisk clip to catch up with him.

I wasn't fast enough. DeWitt's mother was waiting

for him at the top of the stairs by the sanctuary door. I looked around, but there was no Mr. Clauson in sight. Mrs. Clauson's pink hat and dress and white gloves seemed to be as spanking new as DeWitt's suit. She really didn't look much like DeWitt, I thought. Her face was round where his was narrow, and her eyes were an ordinary shade of brown. Mrs. Clauson put her arm around DeWitt and walked him into the sanctuary. She had a fierce, blind smile on her face. No one came up to the Clausons to talk to them, but Mrs. Clauson kept smiling to the air.

Aunt Zona was already in our usual pew. As I sat down next to her, she whispered, "Can you believe it, Billy Lou? The colored church isn't good enough for those Clausons. They're going to move right up the ladder with the rest of us."

The Clausons had sat down in a pew near the front. All through the service, they opened their hymnals when everybody else did and put them in the rack when everybody else did. They listened to Reverend Hardcastle's sermon without ever looking to the left or right. When the recessional hymn was played, the Clausons filed out of the sanctuary along with everyone else. Nobody seemed to pay any attention to them, but somehow or other there were always several extra inches of space on all sides of the Clausons. They walked along in their own private pocket of air.

As Aunt Zona and I stood in line to shake hands with Reverend and Mrs. Hardcastle, the Clausons were a couple of places ahead of us.

I couldn't wait to see what Mrs. Hardcastle would say to DeWitt on his way out.

As it turned out, she didn't say anything. She looked right through him. But Mrs. Hardcastle said to De-Witt's mother, "It's always nice to have visitors here at New Jerusalem Baptist. Especially when they go so far out of their way to come see us."

Mrs. Clauson's smile tightened to the breaking point. DeWitt looked perfectly blank, as if he wasn't listening to Mrs. Hardcastle at all. Still smiling, Mrs. Clauson said, "Thank you for making us feel so welcome." Then the Clausons walked down the church steps without once looking back.

Aunt Zona said loudly, "Well, can you beat that!"

·Chapter Four·

T HE CLAUSONS NEVER came back to our church.
Whether they returned to their own church at
Fifteenth and Paseo or just gave up going altogether, I
had no idea. After a couple of Sundays, the talk at New
Jerusalem died down, and the Clausons were mostly
forgotten.

Meanwhile, I was learning that becoming a cool was
complicated. A lot more complicated than I'd thought
at first. It wasn't just that you carried a clipboard and
wore white socks and midnight-blue sweaters. No matter
what happened to you, you had to *act* like a cool. For me,
that wasn't so easy.

These days I walked into the gym every morning
with what felt like a stomach full of cold Jell-O. Mr.
Sharp seemed to have his own idea of what a cool was,
though he would never have used that word. Mr. Sharp
would have said Real Boy. Whatever a Real Boy was, it
was obvious that I wasn't one.

To begin with, I couldn't remember my number.
During the first week of school, Mr. Sharp had given
every kid a roll-call number. At the beginning of each
class, Mr. Sharp had us all count off. That was his way

35

of taking attendance. If your number wasn't called, Mr. Sharp marked you absent. If it turned out that you weren't absent after all and had just missed your number, Mr. Sharp called you up in front of the class and gave you several whacks on the behind with a paddle.

Mr. Sharp's paddle really hurt. He had drilled a lot of little holes in it, so that the swatting stung that much more. I got paddled three times in the first month. I had to swallow hard to keep from crying out. Each time, Mr. Sharp's eyes glinted at me afterward, and he'd say, "Now go back to your place, Lamb, and try to act like a Real Boy."

Not that I was the only one to get paddled. DeWitt Clauson got paddled once. When Mr. Sharp finished with him, DeWitt just walked casually back to his place in line. His face stayed as smooth and blank as taffy.

DeWitt was always like that, even when Mickey Blake and his buddies hummed "Old Black Joe" as he walked into the locker room. DeWitt calmly went to his locker and started to turn the dial on his combination lock. He didn't glance over his shoulder. His hand didn't tremble. Nothing.

Sometime in October Mr. Sharp chose four guys to be captains for touch football. Every single one of those guys was a big cool, like David Lear. David was the first kid in the class to have a mustache you could really see. It was right there on his face for days before he shaved it off, and of course, shaving was pretty cool in itself. He had zits on his shoulders, too, before anyone else did. Not that having zits was cool, but David seemed almost proud of his, and that made *him* cool even if the zits weren't.

I was on David's team, and he made a point of choosing me last. Well, naturally. A few days before, I had made the mistake of tagging someone on my own side during a practice session. Anyone could tell I would not be an asset in a real game.

David chose DeWitt somewhere in the middle. He didn't make a fuss about it. He didn't grin at DeWitt, and didn't make farting noises at him either, like Mickey Blake and his buddies. He just slipped him into the line-up and then appeared to forget all about him. Somehow that seemed worse to me than being treated like a greaser, or even a dip.

The worst part of all was that DeWitt never seemed to mind. He never showed an emotion of any sort. To me, DeWitt Clauson began to seem weightless, almost transparent. Half there. The Phantom of Emerson Junior High. I just couldn't figure him out.

Then one day the explosion came.

It started one morning after a particularly rough scrimmage. Mickey Blake and a few of the other guys kept tackling kids, even though they knew the game was supposed to be touch. That really steamed Mr. Sharp, but he seemed to get angriest at the guys who were tackled.

"Now, I know it's hard at your age to concentrate," Mr. Sharp barked at everyone. Guys pawed and stamped the dirt like horses while he stared us down, fists on his hips. "You're starting to have bad dreams at night. Fuzz

37

growing on different parts of your body. Little things like football rules just don't stick to your skulls." Now Mr. Sharp was focusing his steely eyes on me. I was trying not to rub my knees, which were skinned and raw from being tackled by Mickey Blake. "You take Lamb here. He may not know the rules, but he works his little tail off on the field. Doesn't accomplish a durn thing, but that doesn't matter to him. Isn't that right, Lamb?"

I kept my eyes on my sore knees.

"You boys have got to learn to *listen*. You've got to learn to *think* about what you're doing. That's what the game of life is all about. You think hard, and then you follow those *rules*." By now Mr. Sharp was bellowing. Everyone on the field grew very still. "All right. I'll give you something to think about. Everybody — ten laps around the track! Now!"

I tried to stifle a moan. Ten laps were bad enough when your knees were perfectly fine, but mine were killing me every time I even set my feet down.

Mr. Sharp heard me. "What's the matter, Lamb? Ten laps too rough for those delicate feet? A Real Boy takes his medicine. You'll do *twelve* laps."

My mouth dropped.

Mr. Sharp's eyes flashed. He was daring me to say something. I think he wanted an excuse to bring the paddle out.

I bit my lip.

We started running. The only other person who took as long as I did to get around the track was DeWitt

Clauson. DeWitt only had to run ten laps, but he ran them as if he were underwater. He ran the way people sometimes do in dreams, with a very slow, graceful motion, and the look on his face was a dreamer's look, too. Empty and faraway.

That's how DeWitt and I happened to be the last two to get back to the locker room. DeWitt made it a few steps ahead of me, so I was the very last one in. Every breath was a gasp. My legs wobbled, and I had to hold on to doors, to windowsills, to walls, in order to walk straight. It was only the end of first hour. I didn't know how I could last until the end of the day.

Just inside the door, I had to stop again and steady myself against the door frame. From there I saw the whole thing.

DeWitt had just gotten to his locker, and had started to peel off his gym suit. But the lock was gone, and there was a big dent in his locker door. Someone had painted a sloppy red swastika on the front with what looked like fingernail polish. It was still wet.

The dented door swung slowly open. Even from twenty feet away I could smell the garbage. Old rotten bananas. Orange peels. Coffee grounds. Dog food. Greenish-brown smears that I couldn't identify, and didn't want to. All over the locker, all over DeWitt Clauson's books, all over his clothes, all over everything.

The whole class was holding its breath.

DeWitt shook. His fists clenched. He didn't seem to realize that his gym clothes had dropped to the floor. He was standing there naked and shaking. Suddenly his arm darted out and slammed the locker door shut. Then he opened it and slammed it again, harder. Then again, harder still.

The bangs shattered the locker room like rifle shots.

Mr. Sharp came running. Within seconds he was holding DeWitt from behind and everyone was talking at once. I moved into the room. Odd. I wasn't out of breath anymore.

The second-period bell rang.

Mr. Sharp yelled into the commotion, "You boys. Keep moving. Go on to your next class. This matter will be taken care of."

One by one, guys began to inch toward the door. Mickey Blake and his friends were among the first to leave. I didn't see how they could have had the time, but they had to be the ones who'd ruined DeWitt's locker. At the very least, they'd put someone else up to it. It must have happened while we were outside running around the track. Maybe other kids in the class knew about it, too. I felt sick. As he passed me, Mickey Blake turned and made a fish face. His lips puckered in and out and his eyes crossed.

I stared right through him.

Mr. Sharp snapped, "Lamb. Get a move on." He had let go of DeWitt. DeWitt had picked up his gym suit and was just staring at his locker.

"Are you all right, son?" Mr. Sharp touched De-Witt's shoulder. DeWitt shook his hand away and put his gym suit back on.

"Come on, Louis. Get dressed and I'll walk you."
Paul had come up next to me.

"Wait. Somebody ought to help DeWitt."

"Mr. Sharp will do it. If we hang around here, we'll just get into trouble."

Mr. Sharp was guiding DeWitt into the coaches' office. He was like a basketball guard, not actually touching DeWitt, but pruning his movements so that DeWitt couldn't help but end up in the chair by Mr. Sharp's desk. The office door closed.

"Louis! Second hour is starting. We'll both be late."

"You go on," I told Paul.

Paul gave me a puzzled look. "Okay," he said at last, and went out the door.

Maybe Paul was right. Maybe I'd get into trouble. Maybe it wasn't the kind of thing that a cool would do. But I had to do something to help DeWitt. I couldn't just walk away from something like this. I got dressed as fast as I could. The kids in the second-hour gym class were already filing in. A bunch of them were standing around DeWitt's locker, pointing and whispering. I pushed by them and went to the sink. I set my books down on the floor next to it and began to wet handfuls of paper towels.

I went back to DeWitt's locker and did my best to wipe off his clothes. I didn't try to clean off his books or the walls of the locker. That would be destroying evidence. But DeWitt had to have something besides a gym suit to wear, even if he decided to go straight home.

By the time Mr. Sharp led DeWitt out of the office,

41

I'd made his shirt and slacks halfway presentable. They were damp now and still smelly, but the worst of the stains were off.

Mr. Sharp looked me up and down. He started to say something, then he must have thought better of it. Instead, he turned to the crowd of second-hour kids that were collecting and hustled them to their lockers.

DeWitt still looked shaken. "You don't have to do that," he said flatly.

"I want to," I said. "I — owe you one."

DeWitt stiffened. "You don't owe me anything."

"I want to anyway," I said.

DeWitt picked up his underpants with two fingers. I hadn't been able to do much to save them.

"I guess you'll have to go without," I said.

DeWitt gave a croak of a laugh. "My mama would shoot me if she knew I was running around Emerson Junior High School without my underwear."

I didn't know whether to smile or not. "Aunt Zona would do the same to me," I said.

DeWitt stripped off his gym suit and pulled on his shirt and his pants.

"Are you going home?" I asked softly.

"Later," DeWitt said. "First I have to go see Mr. Reilly. He might call the police. Not that it would do any good." DeWitt sounded bitter. It struck me that this was the most feeling I'd ever heard in his voice. He bent over and started wiping off his shoes with a couple of the cleaner paper towels.

"I'm really sorry," I said.

"Why should you be sorry?" DeWitt said without looking up. His reflection was beginning to materialize in his shoes.

"Because it's not fair!" I shouted. "Because there's no way for you to fight back. Because I — like you." My voice trailed off. Definitely an uncool thing to say. Good thing no cools were around to hear it. But I realized that it was true. I didn't know quite why I liked DeWitt, but I did.

"You don't have to like me. I don't have to like you." DeWitt crumpled up the paper towels and threw them on the floor.

"I like you, just the same," I said stubbornly.

DeWitt had started for the door. I went back to the sink, grabbed my books, and headed after him. "I'll walk you to Mr. Reilly's office."

DeWitt gave me one of his ice-blue looks. I thought for a second he would tell me to get lost. Then his shoulders settled and he let out a long, low sigh. "Okay," DeWitt said. "It's a free country. Or so they tell me."

We walked to the front office together.

· Chapter Five ·

THAT WAS ONE of the longest school days of my life. After I dropped DeWitt off at Mr. Reilly's door, my knees began to hurt again. I felt exhausted. In fact, I fell asleep in Spanish class and again in Social Studies.

When I got home that afternoon, I went straight to my room and didn't come out until suppertime. At first I thought I'd take my journal out and write about what had happened in gym class. I sat at my table, little trails of sweat tickling the back of my neck, and tried to get some words down. Nothing came. After twenty minutes or so of sitting there, I decided that writing wasn't what I really wanted to do anyway.

I put my journal away and stretched out on the bed for the nap I'd been planning all day. My sore knees throbbed.

But now I couldn't fall asleep.

My eyes felt unusually tender, as if even the sigh of late afternoon air coming through my windows could sting them.

Finally I drifted into a sort of blank state that wasn't sleeping and wasn't waking, and I stayed that way until

Aunt Zona called, "Soup's on!" from the breakfast room in the kitchen.

All through supper, Aunt Zona chatted brightly about how she'd been revising her divinity recipe so that she could make it cheaper. I barely grunted at her. I kept my eyes focused on the Clausons' backyard outside the breakfast room window. On an old dying elm tree right across from our table. I wondered what DeWitt was doing. How he was feeling.

"Billy Lou, you've hardly touched that good meat loaf," Aunt Zona said. Her chair made a bass complaining noise against the linoleum as she backed it away from the table. She took her plate to the sink and began scraping it. "At least eat your carrots. You need to build up your eyesight for all your studies."

I looked down at my carrots. Then I stood up. "I'm through," I said.

I was out of the room before Aunt Zona could stop me.

I went to the living room and snapped on the television. The news was on. I didn't intend to watch it, but the noise would make a good cover for what I was going to do. In the kitchen Aunt Zona started her speech about how growing boys who didn't eat properly could get rickets. She stayed on that for several minutes while she scraped my plate. Then I heard the rush of water in the sink, and I knew it was safe to sneak out the front door.

Aunt Zona would be wrapped up in the dishes for a good twenty minutes. That would probably give me time to get over to the Clausons' and back. I didn't want a lot of questions from Aunt Zona about where I was going and why. I could be pretty sure that Aunt Zona wouldn't like my paying the Clausons a visit, even if she knew what had happened to DeWitt at school.

Come to think of it, Paul wouldn't like my going to DeWitt's house either. He always acted as if DeWitt had some kind of disease. Not to mention what cools like David Lear would think. But there was no reason why the cools ever had to find out about it.

As I crossed the lawn to the Clausons', I heard the muffled sound of someone singing. It wasn't a song. It wasn't even a tune. It was just someone's voice going up and down scales. As I walked up the Clausons' porch steps, the voice got louder. Was it a man's voice or a woman's? I couldn't tell.

My palms felt clammy. I didn't know yet just what I wanted to say to DeWitt. *Hi. Feeling better?* That sounded like something you'd say to someone who'd just had a small dizzy spell. What did you say to someone who'd had garbage smeared all over his belongings?

Still, I didn't want to turn back. I pressed the doorbell. My finger left an oblong damp spot on the black button.

The singing went on. No one came to the door.

I pressed the bell again. This time I leaned on it.

The singing stopped, then started up again. But a minute later I heard someone fiddle with the lock on the other side of the front door. It opened halfway, and Mrs. Clauson stood in the gap.

46

"Yes?" Mrs. Clauson sounded polite, but not exactly friendly. I wondered if she even recognized me.

"It's Louis, from next door. I'm in some of DeWitt's classes at school."

Mrs. Clauson nodded. "DeWitt has mentioned you," she said.

"I'm sorry to bother you, but I was just wondering how DeWitt was getting along. I mean, I saw what happened at school today, and I was . . . just wondering." I was beginning to feel really stupid. What was I doing here? After all, DeWitt himself had said, "You don't have to like me. I don't have to like you."

Mrs. Clauson pulled the door open a little wider, as if to get a better look at me. Inside, the singing stopped again. "I'm afraid DeWitt is busy right now. This is his practice time."

"Who is it, Mama?" DeWitt appeared behind Mrs. Clauson. "Oh, hi." He was already back to his usual aloof, expressionless self.

I flushed. "I just thought I'd see how you were doing."

DeWitt flung out both arms dramatically. "All in one piece," he said. "No additional mess to pick up."

"DeWitt," Mrs. Clauson said sharply. "This young man very kindly dropped by to express his concern. There is no need for sarcasm." Then her voice shifted back to polite: "Won't you come in for a moment?"

I backed up an inch. "Maybe some other time, if you're busy."

"No. Really. Come in," DeWitt said. This time he

didn't sound aloof or dramatic. He just sounded tired. He looked it, too, as tired as I felt.

I stepped into the Clausons' living room. All of the furniture looked either new or expensive or both. There was the crystal lamp I'd seen Mrs. Clauson carrying the day they moved in. There was a wine-colored Oriental rug with touches of gold and turquoise. There was an overstuffed brown velvet couch that looked as if no one had ever sat on it.

Mrs. Clauson waved me over to the couch.

The cushions wheezed faintly as I lowered myself onto them. "This is very nice furniture," I said.

"What did you expect? Orange crates?" DeWitt said. Then he caught his mother's eye. "Sorry. I guess I'm still not in the greatest of moods."

Mrs. Clauson said, "Good manners don't wait upon good moods. But" — and here she smiled for the first time — "I think Louis will forgive us if we're not at our best tonight. It's been a pretty trying day."

"I know what you mean!" I said.

"Would you care for some limeade? I think DeWitt has time for a short break."

"Okay," I said. I hated limeade, but now wasn't the time to mention that.

Mrs. Clauson left the room.

I swallowed. "Um." I cast around the room, trying to think of something to talk about besides what had happened at school. "So you sing?"

DeWitt sat down on the Oriental rug and crossed his

48

legs under him. "That's right. My mama intends for me to become the next Paul Robeson."

"Who?"

"A famous Negro singer. Only Robeson is a bass and I'm a tenor." DeWitt shrugged.

"You take special lessons?"

"For five whole years now. With a tutor at the Conservatory of Music. I've got a big recital coming up in December. You better move fast, or Mama'll try to sell you a ticket."

"That would be okay," I said. "I might come. What kind of stuff do you sing?"

"The works. Opera, church music, even a few show tunes. Mama's so excited about this recital she might even invite my daddy."

"You don't live with him, do you?" I'd been wondering why I never saw Mr. Clauson around.

DeWitt shook his head emphatically. "We don't talk about Daddy unless the alimony checks are late."

"I never even met my father," I said, and right away felt myself turn pink. That was too much to tell DeWitt Clauson. I looked over at the crystal lamp. My reflection stretched out in the base, all forehead and hands and no body.

When I looked back, DeWitt was balancing on his knees. He leaned toward me. "You didn't have to come over here and check up on me. I can cope."

"I know," I said, bristling. "I — "

"But thanks anyway," DeWitt interrupted. "And

thanks for helping out this morning. I mean it." Then DeWitt looked into the lamp and I looked down at the rug.

We were sitting like that when Mrs. Clauson came back with the limeade. "So quiet!" she said, handing me a glass. I noticed how the pink of her palm shaded into the light tan of the back of her hand. "DeWitt, why don't you show Louis what you've been working on?"

"Oh, Mama," DeWitt groaned.

"I'm sure Louis would be very interested in your re-cital plans," Mrs. Clauson said to the top of his head. "Wouldn't you, Louis?"

"Oh, yes," I said quickly. DeWitt spluttered. "No, I really would!"

DeWitt looked at me and I looked at DeWitt. Then we both smiled shyly. Something had changed between us since this morning. We had crossed some kind of line.

"Okay," DeWitt said. "Come on back."

I stood up and forced down a gulp of limeade, trying more or less successfully not to make a face at the taste. DeWitt and Mrs. Clauson led me back to a small room off the kitchen that had nothing in it but an upright piano, a piano bench, and a bookcase filled with stacks and stacks of sheet music.

"Sing the Schubert for us," Mrs. Clauson prompted.

"Oh, Mama, not the Schubert. That's too serious!" DeWitt plopped down on the piano bench and dangled his hands between his knees. "I'm not up to that."

"All right, then. You pick."

DeWitt got up slowly. He rummaged around in the

bookcase for a few seconds. "This one." DeWitt handed some music to his mother.

"The Schubert is so lovely," she murmured. But she sat down and began to play a lively introduction.

DeWitt's voice filled the room:

> "I never cared much for moonlit skies,
> I never wink back at fireflies,
> But now that the stars are in your eyes,
> I'm beginning to see the light."

DeWitt's whole face changed. Now he didn't look tired or even serious. His eyes sparkled and his chin was cocked at a jaunty angle. You would have thought Ed Sullivan had just called his name on national television.

The best part was DeWitt's voice. He didn't just sing the words, he played with them. His voice took little side roads away from the melody, then came back to it as if touching base. He had a strong voice: high-pitched for a boy, but not thin or girlish.

When he finished, I started applauding with my drink in one hand. The ice in my limeade clinked for emphasis. I wasn't just being polite. He deserved it. Mrs. Clauson joined in, beaming.

DeWitt rolled his eyes impatiently, but he did look a little pleased.

"That was one of my encores," DeWitt explained. "After all the serious stuff, I do Duke Ellington and Fats Waller and people like that. My teacher says audiences eat up that kind of thing."

"Of course," Mrs. Clauson said, shuffling the music at the piano, "our goal is still to become a *classical* singer." She said it just a little too loud.

DeWitt threw me an exasperated look behind her back. "Mama's already reserved herself a box at the Metropolitan Opera in New York City for my debut," he said dryly.

Mrs. Clauson stood up. "Well, Louis," she said, ignoring him, "it's time for DeWitt to get back to work. Is something wrong with your limeade?"

I'd only taken that one swallow, so my glass was still full. I slurped into it, hoping that I sounded enthusiastic, but not wanting to actually get too much limeade in my mouth. "It's fine," I said. "I'm just in kind of a hurry."

I was, too. Aunt Zona would be down to scrubbing out the oven by now. If I didn't hotfoot it back home, she'd be sure to start wondering where I was.

I gave the glass back to Mrs. Clauson. "Thank you very much," I said. I glanced at DeWitt. "Maybe we could walk to school together sometime. Like tomorrow, for instance."

"Maybe we could," DeWitt said.

The Clausons saw me to the door. I leaped down the porch steps and dashed across the lawn. As I reached our own porch, it hit me that if DeWitt and I walked to school together, either Aunt Zona or one of the cools at Emerson would be bound to notice. But right now I didn't care what anybody thought. My mind was made up about one thing.

I wanted to know DeWitt Clauson better.

· Chapter Six ·

THEY NEVER FOUND out who messed up DeWitt's locker. I had my hunches, of course, and so did DeWitt, but we couldn't prove anything. Mickey Blake's crowd were experts at looking dumb and innocent, and nobody would admit to having seen Mickey or any of his friends at the locker.

One nice thing: Mr. Reilly paid for a new set of textbooks for DeWitt out of a school emergency fund. DeWitt didn't seem very impressed, but he did write Mr. Reilly a thank-you note. He told me later his mother made him.

For a few days DeWitt got a lot of funny looks whenever he walked into gym class. Some of the guys acted as if they were afraid of DeWitt, as if he might haul off and do something shocking to get even. Of course, DeWitt never did anything, and pretty soon everyone was treating him normally again. That is, most of the kids went back to ignoring him.

DeWitt and I were walking to school together practically every morning now. Aunt Zona was sure to have something to say about that, but I had fixed it so she probably wouldn't find out for a while. I always asked

DeWitt to meet me on the corner. I was afraid DeWitt knew perfectly well why I wanted to do that, but if he minded, he didn't say so.

DeWitt was warming up a little. The first few times we walked to school together, he hardly spoke. I asked him lots of questions about his music to keep the conversation going. But gradually, we found other things to talk about, things at school. It wasn't long before we were able to laugh and joke some, the way Paul and I did. Or the way Paul and I used to.

I still walked home with Paul most afternoons, but it wasn't like before. When we tried to talk, there were these awkward silences, and then one of us would let out a spurt of nervous giggles. It wasn't that we had stopped liking each other, exactly. It just seemed that now we had to work at liking each other.

On the other hand, it got easier and easier to like De-Witt. Not that he was easy to figure out. There were still lots of things about DeWitt Clauson that I didn't understand. Take what happened the day of the cheerleader tryouts.

The tryout assembly was held on a Friday morning before first hour. DeWitt and I walked to the auditorium together. As we threaded our way through the crowd to try to find good seats, I saw Paul just a little ahead of us. I waved. Paul gave a kind of half-wave back. His face wore an embarrassed smile, so I knew better than to ask Paul to sit with DeWitt and me. Sure enough, Paul latched onto David Lear, and the two of them moved way to the front.

I felt a twinge of jealousy. It looked as if Paul had done it. Become a cool. Look at how buddy-buddy he was with David Lear. Paul and David were wearing identical midnight-blue sweaters. Even their clipboards looked identical, both equally brown and battered and messy. I didn't see how Paul's clipboard could have gotten so beat-up and mine could have stayed so new-looking when we'd bought them at almost exactly the same time.

What did Paul know that I didn't know? The way he and David poked each other as they sat down. All their gestures. Everything seemed to be part of a secret code I'd never be able to crack.

But did I really want to? Sitting with DeWitt Clauson was just as much fun as sitting with Paul and David would be. Wasn't it?

DeWitt pointed us to a pair of seats on the side. "These ought to do," he said.

Mr. Reilly came onstage. He blew into the mike for a few moments while the crowd settled down. "Good morning, Apprentices, Journeymen, and Masters. As you know, today we have a tournament in which our fair ladies have the opportunity to prove their mettle. On the basis of their performances in this assembly, you will vote for six of these twenty candidates for cheerleader. And may I add, having seen these young ladies backstage, I know your choice will be difficult. Each is one of the Guild Hall's loveliest flowers."

DeWitt sank down in his seat. "Have mercy," he muttered.

"Cheerleader candidates have three minutes each to perform a routine of their own devising. In the interest of fairness, candidates will appear on the stage in alphabetical order. Let us dedicate this occasion by singing our school song."

Piano chords rolled out from somewhere in the wings. Everyone stood up. I had begun to learn the words to the school song, but I was discovering that it didn't really matter whether you knew them or not. Hardly anyone really sang. Even DeWitt only mouthed. The auditorium filled with a tuneless drone that the piano pounded onto like a hammer on a sheet of tin. Then it was over, all of a sudden, and everybody sat down into the fresh quiet sort of restlessly.

The first candidate for cheerleader was running onto the stage from one side while Mr. Reilly walked off the other.

"Hey! That's Veronica Allison!" I said, sitting up straight. Veronica had taken down the bun. With her dark hair falling loosely to her shoulders, she looked very pretty. Funny, I'd never thought of Veronica as a pretty girl before. She was all decked out in a midnight-blue sweater and a white skirt, with blue-and-white pompons that rustled when she moved.

Vernica shouted, "Well, all right!

"Two bits, four bits, six bits, a dollar,
All for Emerson stand up and holler! Ya-a-a-ay!"

Nobody stood up, but we all cheered. That was just as well. I was pretty sure everyone who tried out would use the same cheer, and I didn't think my legs could take standing up to holler twenty times in one morning.

Veronica turned a couple of cartwheels and ended up in a graceful split. The audience whistled and stamped feet. Veronica blew us a kiss. Then she got up, gave an over-the-shoulder wink, and dashed offstage.

"Too much," DeWitt said.

The next dozen or so tryouts were pretty much the same, not counting the kiss and the wink. Those were pure Veronica. DeWitt and I got bored. We started to make funny drawings on each other's hands with ballpoint ink.

A sudden odd silence in the auditorium made me focus on the stage again. Another would-be cheerleader was running up to the mike. Well, not running, exactly. *Galloping* is more the word. Someone with layers and layers of makeup. Someone who had needle-thin arms and legs and an enormous bust. Ellie Siegel.

There was a loud clank as Ellie's charm bracelet hit the microphone. Ellie jumped like someone who'd just gotten an electric shock. The mike wobbled dangerously for a moment, then settled back.

"Well, all right!" Ellie called hoarsely. She cleared her throat. "Well, all right!" she called again.

Ellie didn't have any pompons, so she waved her arms furiously to make up for it. I heard a few giggles from the audience here and there. I wondered if Ellie noticed.

"Two bits, four bits, six bits, a dollar,
All for Emerson stand up and holler! Ya-a-a-ay!"

57

As Ellie cheered, she launched herself into a cartwheel. It wasn't a success. As Ellie was coming back around, she made a grab at her skirt. I guess she thought too much skin was showing. Anyway, she lost her balance and came down smack on her fanny.

There was another burst of giggles, then the gasping sound of laughter being swallowed.

Ellie was struggling to her feet again. Her whole figure had changed. One bosom had moved down toward her ribcage and was pointing straight ahead, while the other was two inches higher and aimed more or less where Mr. Reilly must have been standing off stage left.

Ellie froze. She couldn't seem to get herself to move. The auditorium stayed at an absolute hush, and the horrible moment stretched out and out. Ellie wasn't really a friend of mine, but I couldn't bear to look at her. At least not for more than a few seconds at a time. I wondered if someone was going to have to come onstage and carry her off.

Then someone began clapping into the silence. It was DeWitt. He was holding his hands way out, and the claps sounded louder than normal. That broke the spell. In another part of the room someone else started clapping. Then I started. Then someone else. Pretty soon half the room was applauding.

It was hardly a standing ovation, but it was enough for Ellie to hide behind. Slowly, stiffly, she limped off-stage.

"Poor Ellie," I said under the last of the applause. "She's still the biggest dip in the whole wide world."

"Mmmmm." DeWitt nodded. "But she's got guts. For my money, she put on the best show today. I'm voting for her, just because she had the nerve to be different."

"Not on purpose!" I said. "Nobody would be that different on purpose!"

DeWitt shrugged. "Those other girls were just so many slices of white bread. At least Ellie is pumpernickel. That has some taste to it."

I couldn't think of anything more to say. DeWitt was the first person I'd ever heard defend one of Ellie Siegel's disasters. How could you talk to someone who would say a thing like that?

*

When I got home that afternoon, Aunt Zona met me at the door with a book in her hand. I was a little surprised. Aunt Zona didn't read many books. For a while she had subscribed to the Reader's Digest Condensed Books, but she said they weren't condensed enough for her, so she quit subscribing. I could tell this book wasn't a Reader's Digest one. It wasn't thick enough.

"Hi, punkin." When Aunt Zona kissed me, her book bumped my elbow. "Your snack's in the kitchen, cooling off. I've been so carried away by this book, I hardly know where I am."

I caught her arm and moved the book so that the dust jacket was eye level for me. *Pray and Get Rich*, it said. Underneath that, several lines of yellow letters marched along telling how you too could share in the endless

59

wealth promised by the greatest businessman who ever lived, Jesus Christ. "Where'd you get this?" I asked.

"Oh, didn't I tell you? I sent away five dollars and a coupon from the *TV Guide* to the Reverend Elmer Jenkins Boswell. You know, he's the one that has that TV show on Sunday mornings, *The Everlasting Hour.* I thought reading this might help me get started with my business."

"Oh." I started for my bedroom. I'd watched the Reverend Boswell a few times on Sundays when I'd been sick and couldn't go to church. He had lots and lots of wavy white hair. The Reverend Boswell believed in Positive Prayer. He said that was like positive thinking, only you didn't have to think to do it. His book didn't sound like anything I would spend five dollars on.

Aunt Zona followed me, still holding the book. "You ought to read this, too, Billy Lou. Do you a world of good."

"Umm-hmm." I was still trying to make sense of De-Witt Clauson's behavior in assembly, and here came Aunt Zona shaking the Reverend Boswell's book at me. All I wanted was to get into my room and shut the door and be alone with my journal.

No such luck. Aunt Zona walked fast. She got herself positioned securely in my doorway before I could touch the door. "Listen to this." Aunt Zona opened the book and started reading out loud. I kept my back turned, setting my things down, hoping she'd give up and go away. Aunt Zona just kept reading:

"'Remember that it was our precious Lord Jesus himself who said, "I am come that they might have life, and that they might have it more abundantly." God's promise to each of us is that if we are faithful to him, he will be faithful to us in return, and he will bountifully reward us with all those good things that are rightfully ours.' There. Isn't that just what I've been saying all along, Billy Lou? The Lord wants my business to succeed. He wants"—Aunt Zona flipped pages rapidly—"'every Christian to be prosperous and happy.' There it is, Billy Lou, in plain black and white."

"That's nice, Aunt Zona." I took my journal out of its drawer and opened it on my writing table. I uncapped my pen and tried to look busy. Take the hint, Aunt Zona, I pleaded silently.

"Reverend Boswell says that Positive Prayer can help any businessman. Or business*woman*. You just take one coin, one small coin each day, and bless it with Positive Prayer. And that coin shall multiply. Doesn't that sound good?"

I didn't answer her. If I gave her any more encouragement, she might start up her little voice again.

"Well." Aunt Zona closed her book. "I guess I'll go dish up your snack." She waited another minute, and when I still didn't say anything, she left for the kitchen.

I hated to be rude, but I just didn't want to talk about Aunt Zona's business again. Besides, I couldn't quite see what the Reverend Boswell was getting at. It sounded like he was saying that if you were a good Christian, God would make you rich. But that couldn't be right. I knew tons of good people who weren't rich at all.

I started writing about DeWitt and Ellie's catastrophe at the tryouts this morning. But somehow or other, I couldn't keep my mind on the subject. I kept seeing the Reverend Boswell's white, wavy hair, only it was like his face was floating against this background of white, rolling mist, and the mist was his hair and his hair was the mist. What if the Reverend Boswell was right? What if Aunt Zona did get rich off her divinity? Why didn't that idea make me as happy as it seemed to make Aunt Zona?

Maybe I was just jealous.

"Surprise!" Aunt Zona was back in the doorway with a plate of sweet-smelling white candy. "Guess what I made for your snack? The first batch of the new, improved Aunt Zona's Old-Fashioned Divinity. You can be my taste tester. How'll that be?"

Aunt Zona walked over to my writing table and held the divinity under my nose so I'd be sure and get a good whiff of it. "Gosh. Thanks," was all I could think of to say.

Aunt Zona looked enormously pleased with herself. "We're on our way, Billy Lou. Like Reverend Boswell says, the Lord will bountifully reward us."

·Chapter Seven·

B Y NOVEMBER, I began to feel that I was in a rut.
I wasn't a cool yet, and it didn't look as if I'd ever
be one. The cools barely even noticed me. Paul told me
that David Lear called me "the little guy who runs
around with that colored kid."

I said, "He's not 'that colored kid.' Lear knows De-
Witt's name as well as I do. We're all in several of the
same classes, you know. And by the way, I'm not that
little. I'd say my head comes just about up to the zits on
David Lear's shoulders."

"You'll never get anywhere with that kind of attitude," Paul said.

Paul had a point. My attitude *was* getting pretty sour.
But what did Paul expect? My name never appeared in
"Knite Life." That was the social column in *The Emerson Herald*. David Lear was in "Knite Life" just about
every week, usually in a paragraph like this:

> Seen munchin' potato chips, sippin' pop, and
> rockin' and boppin' to "Love Potion Number 9"
> were Apprentices David Lear and Veronica Alli-
> son, Phil Andrews and Claudia Hardcastle, Don
> Duncan and Debbie Ann Goodpaster . . .

The same names every week. Except that lately, seen rockin' and boppin' was also "Paul Heart." The only thing I had to feel good about was that they spelled Paul's name wrong, and I felt bad about feeling good about it.

I had to get the cools to pay more attention to me. At least see that they learned my name.

One way to do that was to break into the slam books.

All the girls had slam books. At least, all the girls who were cools, or who ever expected to be. Slam books were like autograph books. Someone's name was written at the top of each page: DAVID LEAR, VERONICA ALLISON, CLAUDIA HARDCASTLE. . . . During class the girls passed their slam books around, and while the teacher was talking you wrote your name and what you thought of the person on every page of the slam book. Then later on the girls could take their slam books into the restroom and compare what everybody had to say about everybody else.

The catch was, you weren't asked to write in somebody's slam book unless you were a cool, or might become a cool, or were at least going steady with the girl who owned the slam book. Actually, there was another catch. If you wrote something nasty, the girl could blackmail you by threatening to show her slam book to the person you'd written about. On the other hand, if you wrote something nice — say, about David Lear — the girl could go up to David and say, "Louis Lamb thinks you have superior intelligence," or whatever you wrote.

It was a kind of public relations.

All I had to do to get the ball rolling was find one girl who would let me write in her book.

I finally settled on Debbie Ann Goodpaster. Debbie Ann was in my Language Arts class. She was a cool, but she was an easier target than most of the other cools. Debbie Ann wasn't a cool because she was a cheerleader, like Veronica Allison, or because she made out a lot, like Paula McVay. Debbie Ann was a cool because her father was a house builder and the Goodpasters had practically the only swimming pool in the neighborhood, plus a gigantic rec room. Everyone said that Debbie Ann had "a sparkling personality." She also weighed 150 pounds.

Debbie Ann was the kind of girl who liked to keep on the good side of everybody. I think she was afraid that if she didn't, kids would start teasing her about her size.

The question was, how could I work on Debbie Ann without being too obvious about what I wanted?

The answer came to me one Friday morning when Miss Pattrick passed back our weekly compositions. I liked Miss Pattrick. She looked and dressed differently from most of the other teachers. A lot of them were like Señorita Taylor, the Spanish teacher, who had two dresses: a brown one and a blue one. She wore the brown one on Mondays, Wednesdays, and Fridays, and the blue one on Tuesdays and Thursdays. DeWitt and I once spent a whole hour trying to decide what Señorita Taylor wore on weekends. We finally decided she wore a bathrobe and did laundry.

Miss Pattrick was just the opposite. She bought all her clothes at Woolf Brothers. Cashmere sweaters and lavender neck scarves and brown alligator high-heeled pumps. She had two-toned hair, sort of like a Chevrolet convertible: brown and gray, and her fingernails were always polished into sharp little red mirrors.

One of Miss Pattrick's big slogans was "You learn to write by writing." Another was "A good composition is like a woman's skirt, long enough to cover the subject and short enough to be interesting." Anyway, Miss Pattrick made us turn in a one-page composition every Monday. She passed it back with a grade and lots of scarlet writing on it on Friday.

On this particular Friday, I happened to see the grade on Debbie Ann Goodpaster's weekly composition. This wasn't hard, because Debbie Ann sat in Row 2 and I sat a little behind her in Row 1. Also because Miss Pattrick wrote your grade about six inches high and enclosed it in a huge scarlet oval.

Debbie Ann had gotten an I—. That was as low as you could get without failing.

Right away I knew how I was going to approach Debbie Ann Goodpaster. I got out a clean sheet of notebook paper and wrote:

Dear Debbie Ann:
Everybody has a talent. I know yours is art, because your slam book has such an artistic cover. I like the way you have different colored

pages in it, too. Nobody else has purple or green pages in their slam books. I know that I for one would consider it a privilege to write in such an attractive slam book. My talent is writing. I don't know why, but I always seem to have lots of ideas for compositions. I have more ideas than I can use. I have ideas just plain going to waste. I think that people who have talents should help each other. They can be each other's protégés. How do you like that word? That's only a sample of all the words I know. Meet me after class if you'd like to talk about sharing our talents.

Louis

P.S. I congratulate you again on your beautiful slam book.

I waited until Miss Pattrick had assigned us some seat-work in our English books so that she could have individual book conferences with kids at her desk. As soon as Miss Pattrick started in on her first conference, I whispered:

"Debbie Ann."

Debbie Ann stayed hunched over her English book, staring at her I—composition as if she hadn't heard me.

I whispered louder. "Debbie Ann." I threw a spitball at her, to make sure I had her attention.

Debbie Ann turned around. Her eyes looked red. No

wonder, I thought. I tossed the folded-up note onto her desk.

Debbie Ann unfolded it with a puzzled look. The puzzled look stayed on her face while she read the note. It stayed there so long that I thought sure Debbie Ann had missed my whole point. Maybe I wasn't being obvious *enough*.

But after a few minutes, I saw Debbie Ann take out her fountain pen and write something on the back of my note. Then she passed it back to me. Along with her slam book.

> *Dear Louis,*
>   I will meet you in the hall. Would you like to write in my slam book it would be a true honer.
>
> > *Luff ya,*
> > Debbie Ann

I was an even better writer than I'd thought. Debbie Ann had caved in right away. She must be really desperate for a better grade in Language Arts.

I tossed the note aside and started right in on page 1 of Debbie Ann's slam book: VERONICA ALLISON.

I wanted to set the tone of my comments from the first. I skimmed over the things other people had written about Veronica. Everyone had said something flattering, so I wrote: "A very attractive girl."

It didn't seem like enough. I thought for a second, then I changed it to: "A very attractive girl with lots of acting talent." That ought to satisfy Veronica.

Page 2. DEBBIE ANN GOODPASTER.

This one was a snap. "A very artistic girl with a sparkling personality." I was really getting the knack of slam books.

For the rest of class, I moved through Debbie Ann's slam book, page by page. Here's some of what I wrote:

PAUL HARTE
A true and loyal friend.

PAULA McVAY
A very warm-hearted, popular girl.

DAVID LEAR
A born leader, and very tall.

Most of the pages were easy ones like that. I looked for DeWitt Clauson's page, but there wasn't one. None for me either. I wasn't really surprised.

The only page I had trouble with was ELLIE SIEGEL. There was absolutely nothing good you could say about Ellie, and nobody else had even tried. Every slam book had at least one Dump Page, and Ellie's was more than likely to be it.

Trying out for cheerleader had done exactly one thing for Ellie. It had made her the most laughed-at person in the seventh grade. If Ellie had set out to become the class joke, she couldn't have done a better job. Now Ellie was far more notorious than she'd ever managed to be in grade school.

Somehow I couldn't bring myself to write any cracks about Ellie, even if that was what the cools would expect. I tried to think of something noncommittal. Finally, just before the bell rang, I came up with:

"A very noticeable girl."

I was just putting on the period when the public address system crackled. "Attention, students," Mr. Reilly's voice puffed. "As some of you know, there has been a rash of unpleasant incidents around Emerson Park. For your personal safety, students are requested not to loiter in or near the park premises. Go directly home after school."

"What's he talking about?" someone said as the bell went off.

Miss Pattrick held up her hand to keep us in our seats. "I think Mr. Reilly is referring to the stories we've heard about people being attacked in the park. There have been rumors of motorcycle gangs and beatings, and of course, teenagers are especially vulnerable. I hope you'll all take Mr. Reilly's advice to heart."

Veronica Allison said, "My father says none of these things used to happen before a certain element started to move into the neighborhood." Without turning her head, she rolled her eyes in the general direction of De-Witt Clauson's seat.

Miss Pattrick's eyes snapped. At first I thought she was going to let Veronica have it. But all she said was, "Class dismissed."

DeWitt's seat was in Row 6, next to the windows. I

didn't need to look at him. I knew his face would be stony blank.

As everyone shuffled to the door, I heard muffled whispers and giggles. A deep, dramatic voice said, "Jig-abooooos." I couldn't tell who it was.

I knew I should walk right over to Row 6 and stand by DeWitt. I wouldn't have to say anything. Everyone would know how I felt.

But I had an appointment with Debbie Ann Goodpaster in the hall. I was on my way to becoming a cool. And that was what I wanted. Wasn't it?

I posted myself in the doorway, waiting for Debbie Ann. DeWitt was across the room by Miss Pattrick's desk. I called, "Let's walk home together this afternoon."

DeWitt gave a shrug that could have meant anything. He didn't answer.

"Hi, Louis." Debbie Ann had caught up with me. She held her hand out.

I gave Debbie Ann's slam book back to her and we went out into the hall to talk about next week's composition.

*

As it turned out, I couldn't find DeWitt after school. He wasn't at my locker. He wasn't at his locker. He wasn't anywhere. So I started to walk home by myself.

Emerson Park looked the same as ever. Why did it always seem so soundproof? You could almost touch the quiet, feel it glide over your ears and down your neck. Today it made me shiver. I found myself walking faster and ended up getting home about ten minutes earlier than usual.

Aunt Zona was at the dining room table, stuffing something into an envelope, when I walked in. "Billy Lou, as soon as you put your things away, I want you to run down to the mailbox for me. I'm trying to get this check off to the printers."

"The printers?" I dropped my clipboard and books on a chair. "What printers?"

"Oh, I've been ordering handbills, Billy Lou. Advertisements. For my divinity. They're going to print up five thousand for me. That ought to get Aunt Zona's Old-Fashioned Divinity business off the ground."

Five thousand of anything sounded like an awful lot to me. "What are you going to do with all those handbills?" I asked.

"Pass them out to people, of course! Just think of all the places. There's church, my bridge club, the grocery store — people always think about candy in the grocery store. There's even your school. Maybe you could pass them out in your classes. Kids love sweets, that never changes. Pretty soon the orders will come pouring in."

I got a quick picture of myself passing out advertisements for Aunt Zona's divinity to David Lear and Veronica Allison. I didn't know whether to laugh or shudder. "But how are you going to fill five thousand orders for divinity? We only have one oven, Aunt Zona."

"Well, I won't pass out all the handbills at once, of course. And anyway, I'm not worried about that part. The Lord will show us a way. That's what it says in *Pray and Get Rich*. All we have to do is trust, and he'll provide the means." Aunt Zona went on and on, and in the back of my mind I could see billows of endless white mist whipping themselves into waves and breakers and crashing across the sky. And Aunt Zona riding along on the crest of one of the waves, smiling cheerfully and passing out handbills.

Aunt Zona was clearing her throat. "Of course, there's kind of a little drawback. I did have to dip into our nest egg to pay for the handbills."

"You mean the insurance money Uncle Emmett left us?"

"It's an investment in our future. Sow, and ye shall reap. Give and it shall be given unto you. Emmett would be thrilled if he knew what good use his money was going to. Thank the Lord he had that double indemnity clause in his policy. Otherwise we couldn't afford to start a new business. You want a piece of divinity before you go to the mailbox?"

I shook my head. For weeks the only snacks in the house had been test batches of Aunt Zona's divinity. It was good candy, but you could only eat so much of it. I was getting tired of going to bed every night with nuts caught between my teeth.

"Well, all right, then." Aunt Zona sounded a little insulted. "It seems to me that someone around here could show a little more enthusiasm once in a while. Reverend

73

Boswell says that faith is the principal and enthusiasm the interest." She handed me the envelope and turned on her heel. A minute later I heard the bathroom door shut, hard.

I went over to the dining room windows and looked out at the Clausons' house. The days were getting shorter. The sun had already disappeared, and I could see my own reflection in the Clausons' dining room windows. It looked thin and pale, like a ghost.

Aunt Zona was going to be mad at me now, I could tell, and all because I wasn't jumping up and down about her divinity business. Maybe she was right. Maybe I should be more enthusiastic. Why couldn't I feel the way Aunt Zona wanted me to feel?

Nothing worked the way it should. Take being a cool. That should just be natural, like being a blond. Why couldn't I be friends with DeWitt Clauson and be a cool, too, and not have to worry about what anybody thought about anybody?

My ghost-self stared back from the Clausons' windows. It didn't seem to have any more answers than I did. I turned away. Right now the only thing to do was go down to the corner and mail Aunt Zona's check and hope she cooled off by suppertime. Maybe later I'd call DeWitt and see if he was upset about Veronica Allison's dumb remark.

For blood relatives, Aunt Zona and I weren't much alike, I thought as I headed to the door with the envelope. Why did Aunt Zona have to be the one with the little voice that told her exactly what to expect? The one who always seemed to know just what the Lord had in mind?

That sure wasn't me. All I knew was that more and more, I knew what to expect less and less.

·Chapter Eight·

D AVID LEAR was even cooler than anyone thought. Early in December Mr. Reilly announced that elections for second-semester Pendragon would be held in January. The Pendragon was the president of the student council. As Mr. Reilly put it, "The good knights strong and true will pursue the Grail of Office." What this meant was that kids in the home rooms would nominate candidates for Pendragon in December, and the five highest scorers schoolwide would get to run. The first couple of weeks after Christmas would be given over to electioneering: demonstrations, campaign speeches, stuff like that.

As it turned out, David Lear was the only seventh-grader to be nominated. This was practically unheard of. All the other candidates — Mary Lou Sinclair, Bob Massey, and the rest — were eighth- and ninth-graders. The older kids probably thought David was some kind of upstart, but if his campaign was good enough, he might stand a chance to win. It was David's big moment.

My big moment, too, maybe.

A couple of days after David got nominated, Paul

came to my locker after school. This was enough in itself to make me look up. Lately I hadn't seen too much of Paul. For all I knew, he spent all his afternoons "rockin' and boppin'" with the cools in Debbie Ann Goodpaster's rec room.

"Hi," Paul said.

"Hi," I said. Then, so that I wouldn't seem to be staring at him, I turned back to my locker and began pulling out my clipboard and the books I wanted to take home. "What's up?" I said.

"Oh, not too much," Paul said. "Except that I've got a new job."

I pulled out my math book. "Is that right?" I said. Then I remembered that I didn't have any math homework that night. I put my math book back. It felt slippery under my hand.

"Yah," Paul said. "I'm David Lear's campaign manager."

I tightened my grip on my clipboard. Paul would expect me to be impressed, and I found I was. Campaign manager was almost as cool as candidate. It meant that Paul and David were really tight. A unit. "Well, congratulations," I said, swinging my locker door shut.

"Thanks. Are you going to support Lear?"

"I haven't thought much about the election. I've been busy."

Paul casually fastened my Yale lock for me and gave the dial a spin. "Well, if you happen to have a little free time, Lear might have a job for you, too."

"What do you mean?" I tried not to sound eager as I shifted my books around on top of my clipboard.

"I've been telling Lear what a good writer you are," Paul said. "He's impressed. We've been looking for a really talented person to write David's platform and his campaign speech. You think you might be interested? It would mean spending a lot of time in conference with me and Lear, of course."

It would mean becoming a cool. That's what Paul was really saying. "I might be interested," I said. My voice squeaked. I hated that. These days that happened whenever I got excited.

"Lear thinks you'd be just the person. Especially since you think he's a born leader and all."

Debbie Ann's slam book. My plan had worked! Good old Debbie Ann, she couldn't help spreading things around.

I fixed my body in the coolest posture I could think of. Knees crossed, slouching against the row of lockers, clipboard and books dangling from my right hand as if they weighed no more than feathers. My wrist was killing me, but I looked just right. "I — " A squeak. I coughed deeply into my left fist, then started again. "I dunno, Paul. I suppose I might be able to put in a few hours every now and then."

"Neat-o!" Paul gave my free arm a punch. "Okay, there's going to be a big campaign party in the Goodpasters' rec room. This Friday night. Be there."

"Right," I said, but I was saying it to Paul's back. He

was already on his way down the hall. "I'll be there," I called.

Paul turned back and flashed the OK sign at me.

My heart was pounding. This was it! I was going to be a cool! I kicked the locker behind me with my heel, just from sheer high spirits.

Señorita Taylor, the Spanish teacher, poked her head out of the classroom next door. "*Ay, muchacho*," she said with a frown. "That's school property."

I buffed the locker with my shirt sleeve. There were no heel marks. I smiled at Señorita Taylor. "*Muy buenos días*, Señorita Taylor," I said, and meant it. Now that I was in with the cools, how could my days be anything but *buenos?*

*

On my way out of the building I ran into DeWitt. DeWitt had been keeping to himself a lot for the past few weeks. He said it was because his recital was coming up just before Christmas. He had to rehearse all the time, he said. Sometimes I wondered if there wasn't more to it than that, although DeWitt always seemed friendly when we did talk.

"Guess what!" I grabbed his elbow and shook it. DeWitt wasn't the kind of person you grabbed, but I was too excited to stop myself.

DeWitt gently lifted my fingers off his sleeve. "What?" he said.

"I'm going to be David Lear's speechwriter. I'm invited to his campaign party and everything."

DeWitt said, "Cool," in a velvety voice that didn't sound at all sincere. Did I imagine it, or did his mouth twitch at the corners?

"Well, it's kind of an honor," I said, and then realized I was hemming. I should have known DeWitt wasn't going to get enthused about a campaign party. As we walked down the front steps, I decided to change the subject. "How's the recital coming along?"

DeWitt sighed. "It's coming. I get awfully tired of singing the same stuff over and over again. Rehearsing's a bore, a big, big bore."

"I guess your teacher's pretty strict," I said.

"Teacher, nothing. It's my mama!" DeWitt picked a twig off the sidewalk and began snapping it into smaller pieces. "That lady is de*ter*mined," he said. *Snap.* "What she wants, she gets." *Snap, snap.* He tossed bits of twig onto a parked car. "I wonder if Caruso had a mama."

A wisp of a smile lit on DeWitt's face like a passing mosquito and disappeared again without a trace. "All I know is, I'll be glad when December twentieth is over and done. By the way, I've got some extra tickets." De-Witt's eyes dropped as he went on: "Do you think maybe you — and your aunt, of course — would want them?"

"Oh, I want them! *We* want them!" It flashed through my mind that getting Aunt Zona to go to a recital where most of the audience would probably be colored people might not be easy. I'd just have to tackle that problem later. "We'll be there, front row center!"

"Ummmm." DeWitt's ice-blue look passed through me for a moment. Then his face went blank and he said, "I guess you and I both are in the big time. Big-time singer, big-time speechwriter."

I laughed. "Big-time cool," I said. But saying it to DeWitt, I wasn't quite sure I meant it.

*

Even though I'd never been invited to the Goodpasters' before, I knew perfectly well where their house was. Everybody knew that. It was the biggest house on Akron Street, just around the corner from Emerson Parkway. The house was set back on a high terrace and had been built a good fifteen years later than the other houses on the block, which were all plain little bungalows with screened-in porches. The Goodpasters' house was split-level.

I'd had a hard time talking Aunt Zona out of walking to the party with me. Aunt Zona had never been in a split-level house before. Besides, she wanted to check to see if the rumors were true that the Goodpasters had a bar in their rec room. I was half afraid she'd make me go home again if they did. But after arguing for an hour, I got off with a promise to be back by midnight and not to walk home by myself.

I kind of wished DeWitt could go with me, just to keep me company. In the old days it would have been

Paul, but the new Paul made me almost as nervous as David Lear did. Oh, well. If the cools saw DeWitt coming, they'd probably lock all the doors. Somehow that thought made me feel guilty again, and I began to walk faster.

I rang the Goodpasters' doorbell, then I spat on my fingers and ran them quickly through my hair. I tugged on the cowlick in back and put extra spit on it to keep it down. I knew I shouldn't feel so jittery. My clothes were okay. I still didn't have a midnight-blue sweater, but I had an old navy blue one that looked almost right. With the light-colored chinos, I could have been wearing school colors. My breath was okay. I'd used half a bottle of Aunt Zona's Lavoris. Even my armpits were okay. I'd used Five Day Deodorant Pads on them. So what did I have to be scared of?

Still, when Debbie Ann opened the door, I jumped.

"Hi, Louis. Come on in," she said.

I didn't say anything. I didn't dare. I might squeak. I just flashed my biggest smile and hoped it didn't quiver at the edges. At least I didn't have to wear braces like some of the kids.

The Goodpasters' rec room was already half full. I breathed a silent thank-you to God that Aunt Zona hadn't come along. Nobody's parents were there, except for the Goodpasters. And the Goodpasters did have a bar. Right now Mr. Goodpaster was behind it, pouring Cokes and Seven-Ups.

"David told me to bring you to the conference room

as soon as you showed up," Debbie Ann said. She sounded very official, like the receptionist at my dentist's. "Would you like a Coke to take along?"

I cleared my throat a couple of times. "Sure," I said in a deep voice. I stood where Debbie Ann had left me while she went over to the bar. In the far corner of the room a hi-fi was blaring. Debbie Ann's hi-fi was red and had detachable speakers. It was the fanciest record player I'd ever seen outside of an appliance store.

I tapped my foot to the music, as nonchalantly as I could. A bunch of kids were dancing. I prayed that no one would expect me to dance before Debbie Ann got back with the Coke. The minute everybody saw me try to dance, they'd know for sure I wasn't really a cool. Only disguised as one.

I needn't have worried. The other kids scarcely glanced at me. A guy from my Language Arts class waved at me sort of half-heartedly. I flipped back what I hoped was an equally cool wave. Since nobody was really looking at me, I could stare as much as I wanted to. I kept thinking that something exciting was going to happen soon, with all these cools in the room. Nothing did. By the time Debbie Ann got back with my Coke, I was down to counting the pairs of white socks I could see. This was easy, because a lot of the kids had their shoes off. Fourteen pairs.

The Coke was in a tall glass with a picture of a cancan dancer on it. BOTTOMS UP, it said in gilt letters along the side. I was glad Aunt Zona couldn't see that either.

"This way." Debbie Ann led me to a little room to one side of the rec room with a cardboard sign on the door:

OFFICIAL HEADQUARTERS OF THE DAVID LEAR CAMPAIGN

The lettering was very straight and bright red. It looked like Paul's work. Paul was a good artist.

Debbie Ann gave a "shave-and-a-haircut, two-bits" knock on the door.

Paul poked his head out. "Hey, Louis! Just the man we've been waiting for!" He sounded lots jollier than usual. I guessed that meant Paul was a good campaign manager.

In spite of myself, I felt a wide, definitely uncool grin start to spread itself on my face. It was dumb to feel so pleased. After all, this was only Paul.

Behind him, David Lear pushed the door open all the way. "Good to see you, Louie. Now we can really get started," he said. David stepped around Paul and clamped a hand on my shoulder. "Come right on in."

"Lou-*is*," I muttered.

"What's that, sport?" David squeezed my shoulder.

"Nothing. I just said my name."

As I took a sip of my Coke, David said, "We all know your name, sport, no sweat about that," and propelled me into the little room.

When it wasn't David Lear's headquarters, the room must have been Mr. Goodpaster's workshop. There were tools and blueprints everywhere. A table and a few folding canvas chairs had been cleared in one corner.

"Thanks, Debbie Ann," Paul said dismissively.

Debbie Ann disappeared.

David sat me down in one of the canvas chairs, then sat down facing me. Our knees were almost touching. A faint smell of Dentyne wafted across from David's chair. Paul hoisted himself onto the table.

For a minute, nobody said anything. David fixed me with a solemn look. "I guess you know how important you are to this organization," he said at last.

"I'll say!" Paul gave me a grin. The old Paul.

I shrugged. As modestly as I could manage, I took another sip of Coke and settled down into my canvas chair.

"This is going to be a tough race," David said.

"Really tough," Paul agreed.

"A lot of our success is going to depend on having an outstanding platform. Not just good, outstanding. And my campaign speech has really got to grab 'em."

Paul nodded. "It's got to be better than anyone else's speech."

David Lear tapped an index finger on my knee. "That's why I personally have chosen you to be my head speechwriter," he said. "Because I know what a wonderful writer you are. Right, Paul?"

"Right."

"I know that with your help we're going to win this election big." David slapped my knee. "I know you're going to do a brilliant job."

It was getting hard to keep from blushing. "I'll try," I mumbled.

"I was hoping we could draft the entire campaign platform tonight," David said. "Mind if I take a sip of your Coke?"

I held it out to him, and he took the glass.

"The main thing is to keep the platform reasonable. Don't promise anything we can't deliver."

"Well, what can we deliver?" I said. "What kind of platform did you have in mind?"

David gave my knee another slap. "That's your department, sport. I'm giving you a free hand. You can write anything you want — with my approval, and my campaign manager's approval, of course. You've got total responsibility in the writing game."

Paul's grin got wider. "See, Louis. We trust you completely."

"Well, good," I said, but my voice sounded weak in my own ears. I didn't have the slightest idea how to write a campaign platform. What if I messed it up? My whole career as a cool would be over before it even got started.

David stood up. "Paul's got some plans for posters. Maybe the two of you could trade off ideas. Work together. I'll leave you alone for a while and go check on the party."

"But — "

David pounded the top of my head with his hand. "Really good to have you with the organization."

Before I could say more, he was out the door.

Paul jumped down from the table. "Okay, you're in! You've got the David Lear seal of approval! This is going to be so much fun, Louis — working together on the campaign. It'll be just like last year, with the King Arthur play, only better. Lear is a great guy, right?"

I felt sort of dazed, like someone who's just walked out of a movie theater onto a bright sidewalk. I didn't quite know where I was or what I was going to do next.

Absent-mindedly, I looked around for my Coke. Then I realized. David Lear had taken my Coke with him.

·Chapter Nine·

ONCE I STARTED writing for David Lear, I scarcely had time for anything or anyone else. "I've even had to give up writing in my journal," I complained to DeWitt on one of our morning walks to school.

"So quit," DeWitt said sensibly.

I gave him a shocked look. "Quit? But I'm really getting in with Lear. Wait until the next *Emerson Herald* comes out. My name will be right there in the 'Knite Life' column with David's and Paul's. This is no time to quit. It's just that I expected all this to be a little more . . . you know, fun."

"Telling me that David Lear's top idea man doesn't have fun? What can this world be coming to?" DeWitt mocked.

I found myself squirming. DeWitt always managed to give me the feeling that I was about a hundred years younger than he was. Besides, talking this way made me feel disloyal to David. I changed the subject fast. Made DeWitt talk about his recital and all the last-minute changes in the order of songs.

But when I got to the Goodpasters' workroom that night, instead of jumping into the spirit of the campaign,

I felt more disgruntled than ever. It did seem to me that a future president of the Emerson Junior High student body ought to have a few ideas of his own. Paul and I shouldn't have to do all the thinking.

"It doesn't seem exactly fair," I fumed to Paul. We were both wearing sweaters because the heat from the rec room didn't quite penetrate into Mr. Goodpaster's workshop. "Here we are shut up in this freezing little room, working ourselves numb, while David's out there in the rec room dancing with Veronica Allison."

Paul dipped his paintbrush into the jar of midnight-blue tempera he'd mixed specially out of two different shades. "You've got to understand politics," he said without looking up from the poster he was painting. "Lear has a responsibility to mingle. He's got to make people like him. Otherwise he doesn't stand a chance."

"I guess that makes sense," I said reluctantly. "But still — "

"Look here. This is the third campaign party in two weeks, right?"

I nodded.

"And we're getting all the free Coke we can drink. We can go out into the rec room and dance any time we want. What's the beef?"

I never wanted to go out and dance, but Paul did it every now and then. I grunted noncommittally.

"You've got to have team spirit, Louis," Paul said. "That's what this organization is. A team. And Lear is the captain. Every team has to have a captain, right?"

I just looked at him. Lately Paul was beginning to

sound like a short Mr. Sharp. A basketball coach without a whistle. Come to think of it, a lot of the cools sounded that way.

I sighed and turned back to the speech I was writing. It was my third try. Somehow I couldn't get past the first paragraph:

> Mr. Reilly, faculty, students, my friends. I speak as the voice of the future. I come to you to bring the Guild Hall into the age of Sputniks and Explorers. Elect me Pendragon, and I promise you a Space-Age Guild Hall. . . .

It all sounded very grand, but I didn't think anyone would really believe it. David's platform was to put candy machines in the cafeteria and to turn a textbook storeroom into an after-school student lounge. Those were the best ideas I could come up with, but it was going a bit far to say that they would move Emerson into the space age. Still, I knew this was the way campaign speeches had to sound.

The door banged open. A rush of warm air, along with a chorus of Annette Funicello singing "First Name Initial," swept in from the rec room.

"Say, guys." David Lear leaned into the door frame. You could see two large spreading damp spots on his shirt, one under each arm. From dancing, I thought, a little bitterly. "How about a break?"

"Sure," Paul said, putting his brush back into the jar. "Hey, David, take a look at this."

Paul held up the poster he'd been painting. It showed a tall kid who looked vaguely like Lear wearing a suit of midnight-blue armor and a space helmet. The kid brandished a big sword with the word *Excalibur* on the hilt. In the background a school building something like Emerson was blasting off in a cloud of smoke. The midnight-blue lettering read:

DAVID LEAR. A SPACE-AGE PENDRAGON.

Paul was trying to make his posters go along with the speech I was writing. "What do you think?" he said.

"Out-standing," David said. He squeezed Paul's shoulder, and Paul blushed. David widened his smile to include me. "We're going to cream the opposition next month. Absolutely *cream* 'em. Come on." David waved us out of the workroom.

Paul followed at his heels. I dragged behind a little. At first I thought David was going to take us into the rec room and make us dance. Like, for instance, with Veronica Allison. I couldn't do that, even if Veronica went along with the idea. I hated to dance, and besides that, Veronica was so much taller than I was that my Adam's apple would brush against her chest in all the slow dances.

But David didn't stop in the rec room. He led us all the way upstairs and out the front door. He didn't stop until we were behind one of the tall, bare hedges in the yard. David looked around, then he pulled something out of his back pocket. A pack of Lucky Strike cigarettes. He held the package out to me. "Want one, sport?"

"No!" It came out in a squeak, and I realized I sounded scared, not cool at all. It was just that David had caught me off guard. Aunt Zona said that the body was the temple of the Holy Ghost, which meant you shouldn't smoke. I'd never been any closer to a pack of cigarettes than watching the commercials on *Wagon Train*. David might have been offering me a machine gun. I cleared my throat and tried to save myself. "That is, I'd better not get smoke on my breath tonight. You know how Aunt Zona is, at least, Paul does — "

Paul and David were busy lighting up. They didn't respond.

I crossed my arms to keep from shivering. The ground was spattered with thin trails of white from a short snowstorm we'd had this afternoon. Christmas is coming, I thought. I hadn't done any shopping. I'd been too busy working on the campaign.

David puffed on his cigarette. Smoke mingled with the white clouds of his breath and twined up into the night air. He didn't look cold at all. Maybe cigarettes raised your body temperature.

"You know what?" David said.

"What?" Paul gasped. He was between inhaling and puffing.

"If I win this election, there'll be no stopping me. I mean, in a few years I can be president of the high school. Then I'll get into a good, I mean a really good, college. Maybe some place like Yale. Or M.U."

I nodded encouragingly. If I was a good audience, David might overlook my not wanting to smoke.

"Then I'll get into law school. I'll become a lawyer and I'll be so rich I can afford a house with two swimming pools. You think that could happen, sport?"

David was looking at me, right at me, and he didn't look mad. I nodded harder. "I don't see why not."

"Then you can run for Congress and have campaign parties in your big old house," Paul said.

"Yeah," David said, puffing.

A thought occurred to me. How come none of David's campaign parties were held at his place? Was it just because Debbie Ann had a rec room? It wasn't the kind of thing you could come right out and ask.

"Your grandma still living with you?" Paul asked David, as if he'd read my thoughts.

David gave a funny, shaky laugh that didn't sound like David at all. "Yeah. In the dining room," he said. For just that moment David made me think of a time when I was sick in bed and I whiled away the days by scratching my fingernails against the wallpaper next to my bedroom window. When I'd peeled away a small oval, I saw that there was a patch of some other wallpaper underneath. A completely different kind. Who knows what goes on with Lear when I don't see him, I thought. I was a little shocked.

Then he took a deep breath and sucked in an extra-large helping of smoke. "Nothing like a good smoke, sport. You don't know what you're missing." And I felt . . . almost relieved. David was a cool again. Still.

"Watch this." Paul drew in a mouthful of smoke. Then he pulled his lips into an O and blew out a series of perfect smoke rings. Somehow Paul kept the steam from his breath from mingling with the smoke and spoiling his rings. The rings widened and widened as they floated to the top of the hedge, only to shatter against the frozen twigs.

"Pretty good," David said, so Paul tried it again.

It was while we were watching the second set of smoke rings rise into the dark that I first heard the noise. It sounded as if someone several blocks away were mowing his lawn with a power mower, but that was ridiculous. Nobody would be cutting grass at night in the dead of winter. As the noise came closer, I recognized it for what it was.

I looked at Paul. "Motorcycles," he said, and a gush of smoke came out with the word.

Not just one motorcycle, or even two. The distant putter was turning into a roar. A gang, I thought. It's one of those gangs.

David, Paul, and I walked out from behind the hedge to get a better view of the street. I was half afraid to move, but I was curious, too. I had never heard so many motorcycles at once.

We could see their headlights now, at the end of the next block, coming this way. They reminded me of a herd of one-eyed monsters like the ones in this book I'd been reading for Miss Pattrick's class: the Cyclopes. A herd of Cyclopes, their single eyes glaring. Crunching up the pavement. Heading toward us.

"Maybe we better go in." I had to shout, practically, to be heard.

David flicked his cigarette butt onto the frozen walk. He stepped on it carelessly. "Nah. Let's watch."

There must have been six or eight of them. The riders were laughing and shouting, but you could barely hear them over the deafening motors. I wanted to clap my hands over my ears. Most of the riders were wearing helmets and black leather jackets. I couldn't see their faces very well, but they looked old. High school age, at least. As they approached the Goodpasters' house — and us — a couple of the guys took something out of the insides of their jackets. Just as they came by, they threw the somethings at the lawn. I jumped automatically. Two empty beer cans landed by the hedge a few feet away.

I was all set to run, but David put a hand on my arm. The motorcycle headlights turned to taillights. The terrible roars turned to drones. The cyclists were moving on. They were turning off Akron Street, onto Emerson Parkway.

When the last cyclist had left the block, Paul and David trotted up to the corner to see where the riders would go next. I was feeling wobbly, but I didn't want to stand on this lawn by myself. I made myself jog up behind them.

I was in time to see the last few cyclists disappear

through the entrance to Emerson Park. It was peculiar. As soon as the cycles went into the park, the streets were dead quiet again. As if the park in its silent way had gobbled up the motorcycles, riders and all. And they were just gone. Swallowed. Digested.

I found myself shivering again. The night felt about twenty degrees colder.

"How about that?" Paul said. He took one last drag on his dying cigarette.

David turned to me. "Was that neat, or was that *neat*!" he said. "You ever see anything like it, sport?"

"No," I said, hugging myself tightly. The shaking gradually stopped.

Paul and David whooped and punched each other. "Come on, let's go tell the others," Paul said.

As we headed back to the Goodpasters' house, porch lights were coming on at a couple of the bungalows down the block. A few grownups had gathered on porches here and there and were talking in whispers. Veronica Allison and some of the other kids from the party trickled out onto the Goodpasters' lawn. Veronica picked up one of the beer cans and held it out with two fingers, as if it were a dead snake.

"You dummies," David called. "Why didn't you come out and have a look?"

An arm flung itself carelessly over my shoulders. Paul had come up beside me. "You guys missed everything, and we saw it all," he howled. "Didn't we, Louis?"

I shoved my hands in my pockets. I knew I was red with cold, but now that Paul was standing with me, I felt warmer. *We saw it all. We. Us cools.* Now that the motorcycles were gone, it was almost cozy to stand here on the Goodpasters' sidewalk with my best friend, my best cool friend, and know that David and Paul and I had seen something nobody else at the party had seen. "Yeah," I said, taking courage. "Where were you guys during all the action? It was fun!"

David and Paul and I grinned smugly at each other, three cool guys who had seen everything, and the fib I'd just told hardly bothered me at all.

·Chapter Ten·

IF IT HADN'T BEEN for the handbills, I'd never have been able to get Aunt Zona to DeWitt's recital.

When I first mentioned the recital, Aunt Zona said since when was I so thick with that DeWitt? I decided now was not the time to mention walking to school with DeWitt and the rest of it. Let her pry the details out of me if she was curious.

Aunt Zona seemed to be above prying today. "We'd just be helping the colored people get rich by going," she said.

"The tickets are free," I reminded her.

Aunt Zona's eyes unfocused for a second while she seemed to rummage around in her mind for more arguments. "It wouldn't be safe," she said next. "Going down into Lord knows what shifty part of town at night on the bus."

"The recital is at the Unitarian church over by the university," I told her. "It's in a perfectly good neighborhood."

Aunt Zona looked cornered. Then she brightened and wet her lips. I knew she'd come up with an unanswerable objection, even before she said, "It would interfere with our Christmas. You haven't started your shopping, and I've got a ton of presents to wrap, not to mention my Missionary Stocking for Sunday School. We'll need every spare minute." Just in case I had a comeback ready, she added firmly, "It's the Lord's birthday, Billy Lou."

And that would have been the end of that, except that two days before the recital the printers delivered five thousand handbills to Aunt Zona.

The handbills came in a large cardboard carton. As soon as she pried it open, Aunt Zona gave me one to tape on my bedroom door.

At the top, big purple letters announced:

AUNT ZENA'S OLD-FASHIONED DIVINITY —
CANDY LIKE THEY USED TO MAKE IT

Underneath was a blurry old photograph of Aunt Zona standing next to an enormous jar of jellybeans in the confectionery store in Armourdale. You couldn't see any divinity in the picture. You couldn't really make out Aunt Zona's features either, but she wasn't wearing her glasses, and her hair was darker and wavier than now. The handbill said that only the purest, finest ingredients went into Aunt Zona's time-tested original recipe and that her candy was full of vitamins and minerals. At the bottom of the page was an address blank that said "ORDER TODAY!!!!"

"They spelled your name wrong, Aunt Zona."

She didn't seem to hear me. Aunt Zona was admiring

the neat purple type. She even admired the slick white-ness of the blank side of the handbill. "I'd say these were worth biting into our little nest egg for, wouldn't you, Billy Lou? I'm going to take a batch to church with us Sunday. Maybe take a few orders for Christmas."

That's when it hit me. I knew how to make Aunt Zona want to go to the recital. "You know," I said casually, "DeWitt told me there'd be over a hundred people at his recital."

Aunt Zona was frowning at her photograph. "Do you think this makes me look like I've got a black eye?"

"That's a lot of people." I pressed on. "Maybe some of them would be interested in ordering your candy." Would Aunt Zona take the bait?

She would. Aunt Zona met my eyes, and a shrewd look passed between us. What she said aloud was, "Do you think this DeWitt might sing some nice Christmas carols?"

"I'm sure he will!" I had to cross my fingers behind my back as I said that. I really didn't know what De-Witt would sing.

"I just love good Christmas music." Licking her thumb, Aunt Zona began counting out a large number of handbills. "Do you suppose I could fit a hundred of these in my red purse?"

*

"This sure is a funny kind of church," Aunt Zona whispered to me as we headed for the Unitarian sanctuary.

"You mean the shape?" The Unitarian church was

shaped like a whale. It didn't even have a steeple.

"I mean, just look around, Billy Lou. I don't see a single cross. Not even a manger. And with Christmas coming next week!"

"There's a holly wreath," I pointed out. "And a stained-glass window." The window showed a budding flower. Underneath, gold letters spelled out:

PRAISE TO THE LIFE THAT SETS US FREE

Aunt Zona didn't look impressed. She tugged at the cluster of red wooden berries on the collar of her green holiday dress. "You'd at least expect to see a picture of the Lord," she sniffed.

Aunt Zona was right, there were no pictures of Jesus. There was a picture of Ralph Waldo Emerson, though.

A brown man with a mustache and slicked-up hair met us at the back of the sanctuary and handed us each a program. Aunt Zona thanked him, opened up her purse, and gave him a handbill.

While he was still puzzling over it, Aunt Zona found us seats. The only other person sitting in our pew was a white lady with blue hair and a double chin. "Try to take up lots of space, Billy Lou," Aunt Zona hissed, giving me a shove. "We don't want to get all crowded in."

The sanctuary was filling up fast. At the front was a broad platform that had a piano and a microphone on it. In spite of the hard wooden pews and the green hymnals in the racks and the stained-glass window, I didn't really feel like I was in church. I felt like I was at a show.

Which, after all, I was. My stomach was quivery, as if I were the one who was going to have to stand in front of that mike.

"Billy Lou, quit your kicking," Aunt Zona said. I hadn't noticed, but my heels were pounding anxiously against the floorboards.

"Excuse me." A large man with very black skin and silvery-white bushy hair was tapping Aunt Zona's shoulder. She looked up, startled. "May I get by, please?" the man said.

"These seats are taken," Aunt Zona said faintly.

The man smiled. "I know," he said. "I just want to sit next to my wife." And he came in, carefully squeezing around Aunt Zona's plump knees and my nervous feet, and sat down next to the white lady with the double chin.

Aunt Zona gaped and tossed me a feverish look. Just as she started to say something, the lights in the sanctuary suddenly dimmed. A spotlight appeared out of nowhere and made the silver of the microphone gleam.

And then DeWitt was walking up to the mike, De-Witt in a tight black tuxedo and a blindingly white shirt. Everyone applauded, and Aunt Zona settled back quietly. Only a couple of tight lines around her mouth made me wonder what she must be thinking.

You couldn't really see DeWitt's accompanist very well. The piano was in shadow except for a tiny light over the music. I knew somehow that the accompanist was DeWitt's teacher. I knew it by the way he nodded at her with a confident smile, as if they had gone through this routine a thousand times before. If DeWitt was nervous tonight, he didn't show it.

The piano broke into a set of short, jazzy chords, and DeWitt began to sing, shaking his index finger at the audience:

"You better watch out, you better not cry,
You better not pout, I'm a-tellin' you why —
Santa Claus is comin' to-o town. . . ."

Everybody laughed. It was the perfect way to start off the recital, and it was Christmas music, too. I began to relax a little. At least Aunt Zona wouldn't feel let down.

With the audience in a good mood, DeWitt went on to slower pieces. Classical stuff. Opera, I guess. Most of the music I'd never heard before, but a lot of people in the sanctuary nodded and smiled as DeWitt started each new song, as if all the tunes were familiar to them. I might not know anything about opera, but I could tell DeWitt was doing a good job. The applause got louder and longer after each number. I clapped as loud as anybody.

Toward the end of the recital, DeWitt sang another Christmas song. The piano became sad and soft, and DeWitt's eyes looked to a spot over the heads of everyone in the audience.

"A-ve Ma-ri-i-a . . ."

The words were in a foreign language, but I didn't need to understand them. I understood DeWitt's voice. His high, clear tones seemed to be pitched to make my skin tingle. The hush in the sanctuary deepened. De-Witt was singing into a kind of well in which the only ripples were the silent shivers of his listeners. I began to feel terribly lonely, and yet happy at the same time. My throat caught, and I had to stop myself from reaching out to hold Aunt Zona's hand.

When DeWitt finished, he looked, for a minute, exhausted. The audience breathed in and out. Nobody clapped, but next to me I heard a loud sniffle. Aunt Zona opened her purse and began rooting through the handbills until she found a Kleenex. She gave me a guilty look and blew her nose.

Just at that moment all the lights in the sanctuary came on. The piano hit some rousing chords, and DeWitt started his "Beginning to See the Light" number. The one I'd heard at the Clausons' house. You could hear the relief in the audience as people began to tap their feet to the rhythm.

This time when DeWitt was done, the applause was thunderous. The floorboards shook. Everyone in the room stood up at once, and people here and there shouted, "Bravo!" I shouted, too.

I sneaked a look at Aunt Zona. She was clapping shyly, like she didn't really mean to but couldn't stop herself. The Kleenex was all shredded up in one hand.

The clapping and shouting went on for a long time. I was so caught up in everyone's enthusiasm that I felt surprised when people at last began to push their way to the back of the sanctuary, one by one or two by two. DeWitt had left the platform.

I caught a glimpse of DeWitt's mother at the back center doors. I told Aunt Zona, "I want to go back and say hello to the Clausons."

Aunt Zona's mouth got that tight look again for an instant. And then, just as quickly, the look melted. "I guess that'll be all right." Aunt Zona shoved her Kleenex back into her purse and took on a businesslike expression. "I'll meet you at the outside door." She straightened up and eased into the flowing crowd. In her hand was a sheaf of the slick white pages with purple printing on them.

I flinched. Now that the recital was over, it was going to embarrass me to have Aunt Zona all around the place passing out handbills for her divinity. It might embarrass DeWitt, too, if he found out about it. I hoped Aunt Zona didn't try to shove handbills at the Clausons, but I couldn't see any way of controlling her. This was the price for getting her here, and I knew it.

DeWitt came up to his mother at the same time I did. At first neither of them saw me. Mrs. Clauson was too busy hugging and laughing, and DeWitt was too busy squirming away.

When the hugging was finally done, Mrs. Clauson turned to me. "He was brilliant, just brilliant," Mrs. Clauson said ferociously, as if she and I were in an argument about it.

"You really were." I grinned at DeWitt.

DeWitt looked properly modest. "It went pretty well," he said. Then, while Mrs. Clauson was being congratulated by someone else, he said into my ear, "I have to go to the bathroom so *bad*."

As we both laughed, laughs that were half giggle, half sigh of relief, a tall, light-skinned man put a hand on DeWitt's shoulder. DeWitt's face went blank. "Hi, Daddy," he said without expression. I twisted to get a better view. I'd always wondered what Mr. Clauson would be like. But there were so many people pushing in around me that I had to give up and move along.

So DeWitt's father *had* come to the recital. I wondered what the two of them would say to each other. Mr. Clauson must be proud. *I* was proud. I couldn't help thinking, "That's my friend." With a kind of wonder that I knew somebody who sang well enough to make a whole churchful of people stamp and shout.

None of my other friends could do that, not even a big, big cool like David Lear. Lear can't even write his own speeches, I thought scornfully. But then I squashed the thought before it could grow. If I wanted to stay friends with David, I couldn't allow myself to think that kind of thing.

Something else struck me. In this whole audience, I was the only kid from Emerson. I was the only one who knew what DeWitt could really do. It seemed more wrong than ever, more unfair. If only something would happen to change all that. I could picture DeWitt as I knew he ought to be, surrounded by a lot of other kids who liked him for his talents and didn't treat him like a freak.

Maybe there was something *I* could do. It was a long shot, but now that I was David Lear's speechwriter, I should have some influence with the cools, at least with David and Paul. I knew the cools already had their minds made up about DeWitt, but if I could arrange it so that some of them could spend a little time with him, they might begin to change their attitudes. The basic problem was just this: nobody but me really knew De-Witt Clauson.

I didn't know quite how to make it happen. It was all very vague in my mind. But it was worth a try. After Christmas, I would think of a way.

· Chapter Eleven ·

AUNT ZONA SPENT practically all of Christmas vacation in the kitchen, baking batches of divinity. Orders had started coming through, mostly from neighbors and people at church. Torn-off order blanks with purple printing were scattered all over the kitchen counters. Aunt Zona was sure that this was the beginning of her path to riches, although so far the expense of making so much divinity had pretty much eaten up her profits.

I got a little sick of the smell of divinity, which seemed to reach every corner of the house, but still and all, I was glad Aunt Zona was so busy. It kept her out of my hair and gave me time to mull things over. How could I get the cools together with DeWitt?

It wasn't as simple as taking DeWitt with me to the next campaign party. I didn't know what would happen if I just sprang DeWitt on the Goodpasters, and I didn't want to find out. Besides, DeWitt would never go to a party uninvited. That wasn't his style.

No, I would have to be sneaky, so that neither DeWitt nor the cools knew what was happening at first. I'd have to outsmart both sides, and that might be quite a challenge.

I worked out the details in my journal. It took me several days, because I kept having to rip pages out and start over again. I finally decided to put everything into an outline. We were studying outlines in Miss Pattrick's Language Arts class, and Miss Pattrick said the ability to outline was the sure mark of a clear thinker.

This is what I came up with:

HOW TO GET DEWITT TOGETHER WITH THE COOLS

I. At Aunt Zona's
    A. Make David and Paul come to Aunt Zona's to pick up David's campaign speech when I finish it.
        1. David has to have speech.
        2. Wait until night before election, so he can't say no.
    B. Have DeWitt already in our living room when David and Paul arrive.

II. Getting DeWitt into our living room
    A. Borrow his pen at school during the day.
    B. Don't give it back.
    C. Make DeWitt come over to Aunt Zona's to pick up the pen.
    D. Call him up ten minutes before David and Paul are supposed to come.
        1. To make sure he gets there first.

III. Explaining to Aunt Zona why DeWitt is in our living room

A. His mother sent him.
B. She wants more of Aunt Zona's handbills to pass out to her friends who
weren't at the recital.
  1. Aunt Zona will be thinking about
  selling her divinity.
  2. Won't mind having DeWitt in the
  house.
    a. Even though he's colored.
C. Only a little white lie.
IV. Discussion
A. Bring up singing.
B. Paul and David will be impressed by
DeWitt's talent.
C. Suggest that DeWitt sing a campaign
song for David.
  1. Have one ready.
    a. Write the words myself.

I read my outline over and over. It seemed as close to
foolproof as I could make it.

On January 11, 1960 — Election Eve — I put my
plan into action.

*

7:50. The doorbell rang just in time. I crossed my fingers, set David's campaign speech down on the dining
room table, and went to answer the bell. Let this work,
I breathed.

DeWitt stood on the porch, scowling. "I don't see

why you couldn't just wait and give me the pen tomorrow at school. My mama's standing next to the piano like a pressure cooker about to explode. She hates for my practice to be interrupted."

"Sorry," I said. "Listen, come on in and sit down for a second. I'll go get your pen. It's in my room."

I let DeWitt into the living room. I realized it was the first time DeWitt had been all the way inside our house. He looked as if he were walking on sponge cake.

"Sit down."

DeWitt lowered himself to the edge of a cushion. He didn't really sit. He balanced.

"Who's that, Billy Lou?" Aunt Zona called from upstairs. She had been up turning the mattress in her bedroom.

"I'll be right back," I told DeWitt, and went to head off Aunt Zona with my story about Mrs. Clauson wanting handbills.

By the time I'd persuaded Aunt Zona to go down to the den and start counting out handbills for DeWitt's mother, the doorbell was ringing again.

"I'll get it!" The dining room chandelier trembled musically as I thudded under it on my dash to the front door.

By now DeWitt's scowl seemed shellacked onto his face. "Hurry up with that pen," he said. I gave him an encouraging smile as I went by. If only he'd stop frowning before Paul and David came in.

"Well, look who's here!" I said as I opened the door.

"What do you mean, look who's here," Paul said. "You're the one who asked *us* ov — "

"It's David and Paul," I yelled back to DeWitt.

David was holding a helmet that was made of papier-mâché and shaped just like a spaceman's headgear, but it hadn't been painted yet. The newsprint still showed. Pieces of an ad for support stockings at Jones's covered most of the top. "Okay, sport. Where's my speech? Paul and I have got to get over to the Goodpasters'."

"Yeah, Louis. If I don't start painting this thing right away, it won't be dry for the assembly," Paul said.

David and Paul came a few steps into the living room. When they saw DeWitt, they stopped short. David gave the barest suggestion of a nod. DeWitt trained a what's-this-all-about look on me. Paul did nothing but study the ceiling, his ears turning red.

"You guys know each other from school," I said with a lame smile.

DeWitt made a faint *p-b-b-b* sound.

I rushed in with, "See, DeWitt. The theme of our campaign is the space age. This is a space helmet that Paul made. David's going to wear it when he gives the speech I wrote. It's all coordinated. Isn't that neat?"

Silence.

DeWitt stood up. "Look, forget about the pen. I've got to get home."

"Wait, wait. DeWitt's in a hurry, too," I said to David and Paul. "He has to go home and practice his singing. Did you guys know that DeWitt's a really talented singer? He's almost a professional."

Silence. David and Paul buffed the sides of their loafers on our rug.

"And speaking of singing —" My voice squeaked. I couldn't help it. "Speaking of singing, have you guys ever thought about how much a theme song would help David's campaign?"

DeWitt walked around David and Paul. I trailed him to the door, still talking. After all the trouble I'd gone to, I couldn't let this meeting fizzle so quickly. "See, this is what I was thinking. After the speech tomorrow, DeWitt is standing out in the hall, singing the David Lear campaign song as kids walk to their home rooms to vote. I've already written one, you want to hear it? It goes:

"With Da-vid Lear the fu-ture is now
And as Pen-drag-on he'll be a wow. . . ."

In the half-open door, DeWitt turned with an ice-blue, disbelieving look. He shook his head at me as if at a foolish kindergartner, and then stepped out.

I followed him onto the porch. "Hey, come on. Don't leave yet, just give me another couple of minutes."

"To do what?" DeWitt said evenly. "Exactly what were you planning to accomplish by this little setup?"

"Setup? Oh, no! Well, that is, yes, it was a setup in a way, but I just thought if David and Paul could spend a little time with you, they'd begin to appreciate you more."

"You think I'm aiming to start me a fan club at Emerson Junior High?" DeWitt asked, a little too quietly.

"Of course not! I just thought — "

"Louis, did it never occur to you that I might want to pick my own friends? That if I wanted to make friends with the likes of Mr. David Lear, I'd be perfectly capable of doing so? On my own." The January moon seemed to make DeWitt's eyes blaze cold. He started down the porch steps.

"Wait." I swallowed back something vague but heavy in my throat. "I didn't — I wasn't — "

"See you tomorrow, Louis," DeWitt tossed back on his way across the lawn. "Try not to swallow my pen between now and then. It cost my mama seventy-nine cents at Kresge's."

DeWitt disappeared into his own house.

It took me a second to realize that my mouth was hanging open and clouds of steam were spouting up from it. I wanted to run after DeWitt. Apologize, maybe. Make him understand. But I knew that would never work, not tonight, anyway. I stamped my feet, more to pull myself together than to get warm, and walked back inside, into the silent living room.

I swallowed again. Probably David and Paul were going to let me have it now, too.

David was tapping his foot. "Look, sport," he said, but he sounded sympathetic, not angry. "We know what you're trying to do. You feel sorry for that colored kid because he doesn't have any friends, and you want us to feel sorry for him, too. So okay, we're sorry for him. Big deal. The point is, there's just nothing we can do for him."

"Sorry for him? I don't feel sorry for DeWitt." My voice sounded faraway. Is that what DeWitt had thought, too? How could I have messed things up so completely? "There's nothing to be sorry about," I said louder.

"Louis," Paul said with a kind smile, "you can't really be friends with him. He's too different. He's not like us. He never could be."

"Here's the picture, sport," David said. "In a day or two, I'll probably be president of the student body. Now, that's an important position. I'll have to keep up a certain appearance, have the right friends. So will my assistants."

The right friends. But I already had the right friends. I had DeWitt — or I did until tonight, I thought with a stab of something like guilt. "What are you saying? That if I stay friends with DeWitt I get kicked out of the cools?"

"I wouldn't put it like that," Paul said. He looked surprised.

In an instant, I realized what I had really known all along. I was going to have to make a choice, once and for all. The cools were never going to change their minds about DeWitt Clauson. I'd thought I could outsmart them, and DeWitt too. Instead, I'd been unbelievably stupid. Stupid, stupid, stupid. I could be friends with DeWitt or be friends with David Lear. But never both.

I didn't need even a second to decide. *Say it.* "I don't think I want to work on this campaign anymore. I don't want to write speeches for anyone who thinks DeWitt Clauson is just somebody to feel sorry for."

"Bup, bup, bup. Now hold on, sport. Let's not say things we'll be sorry about later."

"You always take things so *ser*iously, Louis," Paul put in. "Don't get so worked up."

"I'm not worked up. I'm perfectly calm. I just think David ought to get himself a new speechwriter." There. Done. I let out a long, shaky sigh.

Paul and David cocked their heads at each other.

Paul said, "Be reasonable, Louis. You know we can't find a new writer before the assembly tomorrow morning."

"Billy Lou," Aunt Zona called from the den. "These handbills are stuck together. Come help me."

"Be right there." I was glad to have an excuse for leaving David and Paul. I couldn't face them anymore. "I've got to go. You two can let yourselves out."

"Aw, come off it, Louis," Paul wheedled.

I turned on my heel and went to take care of Aunt Zona.

I was in the den for quite a while. I didn't know how to explain to Aunt Zona why DeWitt wasn't still waiting for handbills. Finally I decided the thing to do was make up another lie. I said DeWitt had had a sudden stomach attack. "It's probably ptomaine. We had those canned lima beans in the cafeteria at school today. But you give me the handbills and I'll take them over to his house."

I figured I could carry the handbills down to the corner mailbox and dump them inside. It wasn't a very good plan, but I was too upset to think of a better one. I wasn't worried about David and Paul. At the Goodpasters' they'd throw together some kind of speech for tomorrow. What really scared me was how DeWitt might be feeling about me now. Maybe in his view I'd done something unforgivable tonight.

Aunt Zona peered at me. "You look flushed yourself, Billy Lou," she said. "Maybe I should run get you a cold cloth."

I waved her off.

As I was taking the handbills through the dining room, I thought of the speech I'd written. I ought to throw that away at the same time, as a sort of last, official act of resignation from the Lear campaign.

I reached out to the dining room table.

Nothing was on the table. The campaign speech was gone. I glanced into the living room, but it was empty. David and Paul were gone, too.

· Chapter Twelve ·

O N ELECTION DAY I was at school at 7:30. I posted myself at the back door of the auditorium. As soon as David Lear came by on his way to the stage, I would see him.

I'd left the house before Aunt Zona could fix breakfast. She'd made me stop just long enough to have a piece of Wonder Bread toast and a glass of orange juice. Aunt Zona wanted to make sure I didn't come down with scurvy or anything.

I'd never been so angry in my life. Angry at myself. Why did I just keep on being dumb? Leaving that speech right out in the open. I should have known David Lear would be sneaky enough to steal it. The thing that really got to me was that Paul had helped David steal my speech. Paul was an accessory. "Accessory," I hissed. It sounded vicious. And to think that Paul had once been my best friend.

I ground my heel against the marble floor. I had to stop David before he used my speech in today's assembly. I'd have to make him give it back. I could create some kind of fuss, get attention. David would be embarrassed; he'd be afraid of losing votes, maybe losing the election. David had to lose now. It just wouldn't be fair for him to win on a stolen speech.

Please let him lose, I prayed fiercely.

Gradually kids began to show up and go into the auditorium. Then little groups gathered in the hall, talking about this or that candidate. A bunch of ninth-grade girls tried to pass out mimeographed platforms for Mary Lou Sinclair. Pretty soon the floor was littered with trampled-on papers.

Still no sign of David.

Around eight o'clock DeWitt showed up, all by himself. Naturally, since I was the only one he ever walked to school with.

For a moment I forgot all about my stolen speech. Would DeWitt still be furious about last night? Would he talk to me at all? I tried to catch his eye, hoping for the best.

When he saw me, DeWitt walked over to where I was standing — pacing, actually — his palm extended. He gave the barest hint of a smile. "My pen, please," he said.

I dug into my back pocket and handed the pen over.

"You look nervous, Louis," DeWitt said.

Nothing about the scene in my living room. Maybe that was a cue. He didn't want to talk about it. I swallowed the big apology I'd been planning. "*Nervous* is not the word," I answered in the same offhand tone. I began to explain all about the speech. "I'm going to wait right in this spot until that dirty plagiarist gets here.

Then just stand back. I'll make that self-centered cheater — "

"My, my, my," DeWitt cut in. "It must be something in that divinity your aunt's been feeding you. All of a sudden you're just full of *plans*. Louis, I don't like to be the one to break it to you, but I don't think you're going to make David Lear do anything."

"Why not? What do you mean?"

"Louis, try to concentrate. If David Lear wanted that speech badly enough to steal it off your dining room table, he certainly isn't going to hand it over now just because you say boo."

"Well, then, I'll tell Mr. Reilly. I'll make him stop the assembly!"

DeWitt put his hand over his eyes. "Louis, Lou-iss. How are you going to prove that the speech David has this morning is yours? Do you have a copy?"

I shook my head. "No, but — "

"And you think smooth-talking David Lear and his associates are just going to have a fit of some kind and admit in front of the principal and the whole student body that they're thieves and liars?"

"Well — " But there was nothing I could say. It was obvious, DeWitt was right. Whenever I thought I could outsmart people, I ended up making a fool of myself.

"Good thing for you that you've got friends to calm you down when your other friends steal your speeches," DeWitt said lightly.

"They're not my friends," I muttered. But I glanced

at DeWitt in a way that let him know I'd caught his drift. DeWitt was really talking about last night and my meddling, telling me it didn't count, that we were still friends after all. Maybe that was as important as getting my speech back.

Just before the 8:15 bell, the crowd of campaigners parted to make way for a line of kids who were moving down the hall. It was all the candidates and their campaign managers, marching in V-formation, flashing smiles at the rest of us in the corridor. There they were, Mary Lou Sinclair, Bob Massey, the whole bunch of them, swooping on the auditorium. Ten jets coming in for a landing. Paul and David were on one end of the line. Paul was carrying a large Adler's hatbox that must have contained David's space helmet. I wondered if the paint had dried in time.

Mary Lou Sinclair's supporters began to chant, "Mary LOU, Mary LOU, Mary LOU." That made the other kids throw back the names of their own candidates. The babble grew louder.

The back of my neck prickled with sweat. David Lear was looking straight ahead, wearing the exact same campaign grin I'd seen at all those parties at the Goodpasters'. Not a flicker to show that somewhere under all that poise there might be a guilty conscience.

David was almost at the door where I was standing. If I was ever going to say anything, now was the time.

A kind of fury fizzed through me like some hot carbonated juice, but I felt DeWitt's steadying hand on my shoulder, and in spite of myself, I kept my mouth clamped grimly shut. David and Paul passed on into the auditorium.

"At least we can boo and hiss when he gives that speech," I whispered to DeWitt between clenched teeth.

"If we're going to do that, we better hurry inside and get good seats," DeWitt said.

A few stragglers were still calling out campaign slogans, but the hall was practically empty now. I didn't know what else I could do. I made myself follow DeWitt into the auditorium to listen to David Lear give my space-age campaign speech.

*

The election results were announced late that afternoon. I was in Miss Pattrick's class taking a vocabulary test at the time.

"Write a sentence using the word *odious* correctly."

I wrote, "David Lear has an *odious* personality." No, not specific enough. I scratched it out. "To betray one's fellow man is *odious;* therefore I think David Lear has an *odious* personality." Better.

I hadn't wanted to vote at all today, but Señorita Taylor, my homeroom teacher, had said I had to. So I'd taken a ballot and scratched out David's name. Over it I'd written "President Dwight D. Eisenhower," marked an X, and handed the folded ballot to Señorita Taylor. Aunt Zona always said you couldn't go wrong with Ike.

"Students, your attention. Your attention, please." Mr. Reilly's voice came out of the P.A. speaker over the blackboard, sounding winded, just like always. "We have a new Pendragon." All around the room pencils dropped and papers rustled. Out of the corner of my eye I sneaked a look at David Lear. He was sitting rigid at his desk, his hands folded, his eyes glassy with concentration.

Please, God. He has to lose. It's only fair.

"Before I announce the name of your Pendragon, I want to say, as your principal, that I was most impressed with this campaign. The professionalism of the candidates and their speeches was outstanding. And the results are equally extraordinary. For the first time in the history of Emerson Junior High, a seventh-grader has been elected Pendragon. I know you'll all join me in extending heartiest congratulations and our mutual allegiance to Pendragon David Lear."

The roar in the classroom was deafening. Half the kids were out of their seats, flocking around David's chair. The other half were cheering and stamping their feet at their desks. Miss Pattrick didn't even try to keep order. Instead, she joined the crowd around David's desk and put out her hand.

So that was that. David won. With my speech and platform.

He won.

When the bell rang at the end of the period, I gathered up my books so that I could make a dash for the door. But my hands were stiff and clumsy. I couldn't seem to grip things. I dropped my pen not once, but twice, and as I hurriedly scooped it up the second time, my clipboard unclipped, scattering pages and pages of homework on the floor. By the time I finally had everything together again, the doorway was blocked.

David and Paul stood right in the center of it, while kids from inside the room and kids from outside in the hall mobbed them, screaming and laughing and jumping up and down.

I sucked in my breath a little and started pushing my way through. I was too mad to say "Excuse me."

I bumped right into Paul.

Our eyes met. Paul started to say something, but I shook my head. I felt suddenly embarrassed even to look at Paul's face. It was as if I were the one who had done something wrong, as if I were the one who should feel guilty.

The crowd opened up an inch or two, and I squeezed through, like a cork popping out of a bottle. I was out in the hall, free.

*

After school DeWitt and I walked home together.

WHY? I kept thinking to myself.

The late afternoon sun was falling somewhere behind a sullen-looking curtain of gray. Drops of winter rain pelted the hoods of our parkas. When one of them hit my face, it felt like cold spit.

Left foot down — WHY — right foot down — WHY — left foot down — WHY? It was a burden to walk. I was exhausted. I'd used up all my energy being angry at David and Paul.

DeWitt kept having to slow his pace so that I could keep up with him. At every corner he'd look over his shoulder to see if I was still there, then he'd take a few sliding steps backward so that we were even again. While we waited for the light at Prospect Avenue, De-Witt turned to me and intoned: "*'The heart is deceitful above all things, and desperately wicked: who can know it?'*"

"What's that supposed to mean?" I said sourly.

"It's a verse I memorized in Sunday School one time. Jeremiah 17:9."

"It fits David and Paul, that's for sure." I tucked my clipboard tighter under my arm. I had to try to keep the papers from getting spattered.

"Look, I could have told you what was going to happen all along. You wouldn't have listened. Just think of it as a lesson. Life is like a college. That's what my mama would say."

I rolled my eyes impatiently. We trotted across the street in front of a row of cars that seemed to be growling at us. "It just isn't fair, that's all. None of it. The way they treat you, the way they treated me. The fact that they *won!* That's the worst!"

"I never saw such a boy for fairness. You gonna get a *ul*cer worrying about *fair.*"

"Well, I don't care. Doesn't it bother you? If people can cheat and steal and still be elected Pendragon? If people can kick other people around and not get punished for it? Don't you ever think about things like that?"

DeWitt said very softly, "Yeah. I think about them."

I blushed and looked away. Of course, DeWitt had to know a lot more than I did about things not being fair. How did he cope? He never talked about stuff like that. Did he never talk about it with anyone, even his mother, or did he just not talk about it with me? I glanced back at him. I wanted DeWitt to let me in on something, something that would help me out of this horrible feeling. Something, I didn't know what.

He just let out a dramatic, fake-sounding sigh. "I don't know why I hang around you, Louis. You're really not too smart, you know? You knock your brains out, but you can't quite see what it's all about." DeWitt's eyes twinkled at me coaxingly.

I obliged him with a bitter little smile. But I was thinking about the cools again. Now I knew what they were really like. I knew I didn't want to become one anymore. Yet I couldn't let them back me into a corner this way, make me feel so helpless. There was still something left, something that would make me feel good again, almost as good as being in with the cools.

Getting even with them.

·Chapter Thirteen·

WAYS TO GET EVEN WITH THE COOLS

I WROTE THE ANGRY block letters across the top of a journal page with my cartridge pen. From sheer meanness I pressed down too hard and the ink blotched in three places. The blotches looked like fat, sulky spiders.

But below the title, the page stayed blank.

The thing was, I couldn't think of any plan for getting even that was enormous enough to make up for what David and Paul had done, and yet practical enough to do any good. Of course I had a lot of wild, silly ideas, like putting itching powder down David's midnight-blue sweater, but I tossed those out right away. Whatever I did would have to be serious. And big.

Meanwhile, I had valentines to worry about. Spanish valentines, at that.

Of all the classes I was in, Spanish class was the one where the most kids went berserk the most often. That was mainly because of Señorita Taylor. Señorita Taylor was what you might call an easy teacher. She never liked to raise her voice at kids. Señorita Taylor never got mad. She just got very, very disappointed.

For instance, one time Mickey Blake redecorated the classroom while Señorita Taylor was out in the hall talking to another teacher. Mickey turned the giant portrait of Simón Bolivar upside down, wrote "VIVA MÉXICO" on all the chalkboards, and reached into the glass display cabinet to pick the little serapes off Señorita Taylor's prize collection of Mexican dressed fleas. This was no easy task. The fleas were real—but dead—and so tiny that I felt sure the Mexicans who dressed them for a living must all go blind before they were thirty.

Señorita Taylor came back into the room while Mickey was still working on the third flea.

Any other teacher would have expelled Mickey, but Señorita Taylor simply stopped short and gave him a round-eyed, watery look. She said, *"Ay, Miguelito! Cuidado!"* Which only meant, "Oh, Mickey! Be careful!"

Señorita Taylor didn't even make Mickey clean up the mess. She just had him sit down while she got out the tweezers to put the serapes back on the naked fleas.

So when Señorita Taylor announced that we were going to have a little party in class the Friday before Valentine's Day, I knew right away that things were bound to get out of hand. Señorita Taylor said that the party would be a lot of fun and educational, too. Besides serving refreshments, Señorita Taylor was going to show slides of the Valentine's Day party she went to when she was a graduate student at the University of

Mexico in 1952. After that, Señorita Taylor said, we could exchange valentines in Spanish.

DeWitt and I decided we both ought to wear crash helmets to class that day.

As it turned out, Ellie Siegel needed the protection, too.

I hadn't paid much attention to Ellie since her big cheerleader tryout last fall. Probably nobody had. I'd noticed a few things, of course. Like the fact that her chest was flat again. No surprise. Even Ellie wouldn't be dumb enough to go on wearing falsies after that disaster in the auditorium. But otherwise, Ellie hadn't changed much. She still wore lots of red makeup and she carried copies of *16* magazine around with her to every class. Occasionally I'd happen to look her way and there would be Ellie, poring over some article like "Connie Francis Shares Her Beauty Secrets" or "Edd 'Kookie' Byrnes Tells What It Takes to Be His Dream Girl." I guessed Ellie was looking for some miracle that would turn her into a cool.

The day before the Valentine's party, Señorita Taylor gave us half an hour in class to write and decorate our Spanish valentines. She set the big, thick English-Spanish dictionary out on her desk and walked up and down the aisles, looking over kids' shoulders and helping them write things like TE AMO MUCHO (I LOVE YOU A LOT) or PARA UNA MUCHACHA MUY BONITA (FOR A VERY PRETTY GIRL).

I was having a lot of trouble with my valentine. Not with the Spanish. That part was easy. There just wasn't any girl in Señorita Taylor's class I would think of sending a valentine to. They were all either cools like Veronica Allison or dips like Ellie. When I tried to explain to Señorita Taylor why I wasn't writing, she smiled coyly and said, "Well, one could always send a valentine to *la profesora*, couldn't one?"

I tried to smile back, but I knew that no power on earth would make me send a valentine to Señorita Taylor, especially with Mickey Blake and David Lear and all the others looking. Finally I got an idea. Send a valentine to DeWitt. He was my best friend now anyway. PARA UN AMIGO BUENO (FOR A GOOD FRIEND) I wrote in big red letters on a heart-shaped piece of white construction paper. No lace for DeWitt, I decided.

Maybe I should say something more, like "For a good *and talented* friend." I didn't know the word for *talented*, though. I'd have to get the English-Spanish dictionary off Señorita Taylor's desk.

But the dictionary wasn't there.

I had to look around the classroom a couple of times before I spotted it. A small group of kids had collected around Mickey Blake's desk, kids like Veronica Allison and Claudia Hardcastle. Cools. They were whispering and muttering to each other, with an occasional giggle floating up through the murmurs like a bubble of air through lake water. And when Veronica Allison dashed to her desk for a minute to get something out of her purse, I saw Mickey in the middle of the group, holding the dictionary with one hand and pointing to something on a page with the other.

Veronica ran back to Mickey's desk carrying several pieces of construction paper and a turquoise pen. The whispers started up again as Veronica began writing. Someone in the group screeched out a laugh.

Señorita Taylor looked up from Ronnie Larson's desk on the other side of the room, where she'd been helping Ronnie with his valentine. "*Más calladamente, muchachos, por favor*," she said mildly. "More quietly, children, please."

The kids at Mickey's desk barely glanced at her. Mickey turned pages in the dictionary, and Veronica kept on writing.

The next day I found out what they'd been doing. In fact, the whole class found out.

Señorita Taylor's Valentine's party started out just the way she planned. For the first half-hour she showed her slides. There seemed to be at least a hundred of them. I kept expecting Mickey Blake to crack a dirty joke or at least throw spitballs at the screen. Nothing. Not a word. The whole classroom stayed quiet, except for the hum of Señorita Taylor's slide projector. Unnaturally quiet, I thought to myself.

Then Señorita Taylor turned on the lights and passed out the refreshments. Peppermint hearts with writing on them — in English — and red jelly beans, red Kool-Aid, and pink cupcakes. Still the class was quiet. DeWitt and I exchanged a puzzled "What's up?" look over Señorita Taylor's head.

Finally Señorita Taylor turned to the big red-and-white cardboard box that held all the Spanish valentines we'd made yesterday. The box was stuffed to overflowing. There had to be a lot more than thirty-five valentines in there. Some kids in the room were going to get more than one. Cools like Veronica Allison and David Lear would get whole deskfuls, I thought, but I wasn't jealous. Let the cools get sloppy about each other. I didn't care anymore.

Señorita Taylor played postman. She walked around the classroom on tiptoe, as if she thought that might make her invisible. Every time she dropped a card on someone's desk, she said the Spanish for "I'm giving you a valentine." I couldn't understand it all, but every few seconds Señorita Taylor said "*tarjeta*," which I knew meant "card."

After a few minutes of this, I began to realize what was wrong. A lot of kids in the room had one or two valentines on their desks. I got one from DeWitt. He got one from me. Like that. But Ellie Siegel had five valentines.

I couldn't believe it. Ellie Siegel with *five valentines?* She shouldn't have gotten any.

A few more minutes went by. Ellie had ten valentines. Then twelve. Fifteen.

Pretty soon even Señorita Taylor began to look suspicious. At the back of the room Mickey Blake was silently rocking back and forth in his seat, looking as if he might jet straight up toward the ceiling at any moment. I sneaked looks at Veronica Allison and Claudia Hardcastle. Sure enough, all the kids who'd gathered around the dictionary yesterday were sitting with their cheeks sucked in, little snorts of air popping out every now and then in spite of themselves.

Everyone else began to stare at Ellie.

She'd read the first couple of valentines already. Now she was looking up at one of the light fixtures, folding and refolding a heart-shaped piece of construction paper. All the color had gone out of her face. Ellie blinked and blinked at the light.

Señorita Taylor paused by Ellie's desk. She tapped the sixteenth valentine against the edge of the desktop. The room was so still that you could hear the little thwacking sounds the paper made on the wood. "I think somebody in this room has a poor sense of humor," Señorita Taylor began.

But Ellie interrupted her. She stood up at her desk and started stuffing red and white construction-paper cards into her Spanish book. A couple of the cards slid off Ellie's desk and landed in the aisle, but Ellie didn't seem to notice. She threw her books and her *16* magazine together, and she ran out of the room right in front of Señorita Taylor.

As Ellie passed my desk, I saw tears streaming down her pale, blank face. The door slammed behind her.

One of Ellie's valentines had fallen not far from my desk. I stretched out my foot and edged it close enough to pick up. While Señorita Taylor put her hands on her hips and struggled for something more to say, I read the card. A UNA PERSONA EXTRAÑA.

I didn't need the dictionary to translate. To A STRANGE PERSON. Someone had drawn a stick figure under the words. It had a huge nose, crossed eyes, and some mis-shapen lumps where the bust should have been.

The bell rang.

Kids jumped right to their feet. Especially the cools and Mickey. They practically stampeded to the door while Señorita Taylor called after them, "*Vengan aquí!* Come here!" Nobody listened, of course.

Mickey was singing at the top of his lungs. "My-y funny valentine . . ."

Claudia Hardcastle called to David Lear, "Hey, what about making Mickey the official court jester, Mr. Pendragon?"

David didn't say anything, but he winked at Claudia. The kind of wink adults give each other when some child is being cute and naughty at the same time.

And then the cools were out in the hall and the rest of us were scrambling to catch up with them so we wouldn't have to stay in this room with Señorita Taylor, who was still calling out things in Spanish.

DeWitt was at my elbow. "I think they went too far this time," I told him. "That really wasn't very funny."

We poked our way through the mob in the corridor.

DeWitt looked grim. He passed me a white valentine card. It wasn't the one I'd given him. This one had a picture of a colored person on it. The person had very dark skin, wild-looking cottony hair, and thick, blub-bery white lips with spit coming out the side. Its eyes were blue, though. Blue like DeWitt's. There was some turquoise writing in Spanish, too. I didn't know what it said.

I didn't dare look at DeWitt. I stared straight ahead as we started down the stairs to our lockers. "That settles it," I said finally. "I've got to get my getting-even-with-the-cools scheme into high gear. Right away! Who do they think they are, anyway?"

As I got more and more excited, my voice cracked. DeWitt cut through my raving calmly. "Count me in" was all he said. But he sounded as if he meant it.

"You want this card back?" I said hoarsely.

DeWitt shrugged.

We turned onto the first-floor corridor and I handed him my books. He held them and watched silently while I tore the white card with the turquoise writing into dozens of tiny, tiny pieces.

*

So now I had someone to help me get even. DeWitt. What I still didn't have was the Plan. The simple, brilliant, devastating Plan that would turn the tables on the cools at last.

In the end I didn't have to come up with the big idea myself after all. Miss Pattrick helped me out.

It was a couple of weeks later, and DeWitt and I were walking down the hall on our way to the cafeteria. Miss Pattrick was tacking a big sign onto the third-floor bulletin board.

ATTENTION, APPRENTICES, JOURNEYMEN, AND MASTERS!
THE EIGHTH ANNUAL EMERSON JUNIOR HIGH TROUBADOR
FEST WILL BE HELD MAY 7, 1960,

IN THE SCHOOL AUDITORIUM, 8 TO 10 P.M.
TRYOUTS BEGIN ON MARCH 10.
MISS MARGUERITE PATTRICK, SPONSOR.
SINGERS, DANCERS, ACTORS NEEDED! PLAN YOUR SKITS NOW!

It was like one of those comic strips where a light bulb with the word *IDEA* on it appears over a character's head. I almost expected to see the letters flashing in the air just above me. "Miss Pattrick," I said. "What about writers?"

Miss Pattrick turned to me with a vague smile. "What do you mean, Louis?"

"I mean, can we write our own material for the show? The troubador show?"

"Oh. Of course, Louis! In fact, I want to encourage as much originality as possible."

"And does it matter what kind of skit we do? I mean, can it be anything at all?"

"Of course, anything!" Miss Pattrick was just about beaming now. "Sounds like you have something special in mind, Louis."

"Oh, I do, Miss Pattrick. Something very special." And I beamed back at her. I beamed and beamed until DeWitt pinched my arm to make me stop.

·Chapter Fourteen·

BECAUSE OF DEWITT, I decided to make my skit
musical. All I had to do was put down my thoughts
in verse and DeWitt could turn them into a song. De-
Witt was amazing. He only needed to hear the words
a couple of times before he started to pick out a tune
on the piano. Almost overnight, we had a song, one
that sounded really professional, that might have been
written by someone famous, like Gilbert and Sullivan
or Paul Anka.

Better still, DeWitt had agreed to do all the singing. I
would do the speaking parts and the parts DeWitt called
shtick: the funny little pantomimes and stuff.

By the Monday before tryouts, Mrs. Clauson had
volunteered to be our accompanist. She let us rehearse in
the Clausons' piano room, and Aunt Zona couldn't ob-
ject to my spending so much time over there because I'd
told her we were doing schoolwork. Which, in a way,
was perfectly true. Aunt Zona was really too preoccu-
pied to pay much attention to what I did with my afternoons. Her divinity business had slacked off since
Valentine's Day, so she was busy mailing handbills off

to people again. By now she was down to second and third cousins.

I practiced my gestures ("Make them broad, Louis," DeWitt coached), while DeWitt worked on polishing up our song:

> Oh, we are the epitome of cool.
> We win the games and really run the school,
> Wear midnight blue and wear white socks,
> We sometimes stuff the ballot box,
> But we are very honest as a rule.
> Yes, we are the epitome of cool.

It sounded great. The cools were going to hate it when they saw me doing my David Lear imitation. My character was called the Great Penwiper. (Not Pendragon. Get it?) David would just bust, especially about the ballot box part. The skit was just ridiculous enough to make Lear a laughingstock, but true enough to hurt a little, too. If there was one thing a big cool couldn't take, it was being laughed at by all the ordinary kids who would see the show.

But DeWitt wasn't so sure. "The song's fine, there's nothing wrong with the song," he said. "But something's missing. The skit's not funny enough."

"Not funny enough! You think the Great Penwiper's not funny? When have you ever seen anything that funny on the stage of Emerson Junior High School?"

"I believe I'll just go fix some limeade," Mrs. Clauson said, and excused herself.

DeWitt refused to meet my glare. "Actually, I have seen something funnier at Emerson, and so have you. Ellie Siegel's cheerleader tryout."

"That wasn't deliberate! Ellie's just the clumsiest person who ever lived—she couldn't help messing up."

"Right. She's a natural for shtick."

"What are you driving at?"

"Look. We've got you to take your shots at the Pendragon and me to sing. But we don't do anything about the Veronica Allisons and Claudia Hardcastles, the cheerleader rah-rah types. They're cools, too. I think we need a girl in the act."

Mrs. Clauson was back carrying a tray with two glasses on it. "I beg your pardon," she said, handing out the limeades. "You already have a girl in the act, so to speak. It may have escaped your attention that your ancient mother—"

DeWitt sipped. "No offense, Mama, but I mean a real girl. You wouldn't want to get dressed up as a cheerleader and take pratfalls in front of nine hundred junior high kids, would you?"

"Since you put it that way, I suppose not." Mrs. Clauson winked at me and went back to the kitchen with the empty tray.

"So what girl did you have in mind?" I said suspiciously.

"Louis, think. What girl has more to gain by getting even with the cools than Ellie? We're doing this act partly because of her to begin with."

It just goes to show, I thought. You could be at a new

school for six months and still not understand the first thing about the people in it. DeWitt had to be educated. "It would never, never work," I told him. Trying to be patient. "First of all, Ellie would never get up and make a fool of herself again in front of the whole school."

"Why not? What has she got to lose now? Ellie's already been made fun of in every conceivable way. Maybe she'd enjoy having the last laugh."

I shuddered. "You don't know Ellie. Any time she's associated with any kind of performance, it's automatically ruined. Last year—"

"I already asked her."

"You what?" In my shock I found myself taking in gulps of limeade before I knew what I was doing.

"I asked her to be in the act. Today after Spanish class. I told her what it was about and that we were making fun of the cools. I told her the act could use a good comedienne."

"But that's—that's—" At the front of the house the doorbell rang. "What did she say?"

"Well . . ." DeWitt motioned me to sit next to him on the piano bench. For some reason he seemed to be enjoying himself. "At first she said over her dead body. I think she thought I was being sarcastic. I had to follow her all the way down the second-floor hall explaining. But we talked for a long time, and finally—"

Mrs. Clauson appeared in the doorway. Behind her, flushed and panting, stood Ellie Siegel.

Ellie's eyes darted back and forth as if she were looking for a fire escape. Without the phony bosoms, her midnight-blue sweater seemed about three sizes too big. Her scrawny arms dangled inside the sleeves. She was wearing red, red lipstick and dark mascara, but the lipstick was smeared and the mascara left rows of eyelash marks like perforations above her lids.

"Ellie!" DeWitt jumped up to greet her. His hand squeezed my shoulder, cautioning. "Louis and I were just talking about all the great cheerleader shtick you can do in the skit. Weren't we, Louis?"

Trapped. That's what I was. DeWitt had railroaded Ellie into our act and now it would all be spoiled. I had a good mind to cancel the skit before we even tried it out for Miss Pattrick. But then again, how could I hurt Ellie's feelings? One cross word would probably demolish her.

Ellie let out a small, panicky giggle. "I wouldn't have to dance, would I? I can't really dance good."

Mrs. Clauson gave Ellie a reassuring pat and disappeared again.

DeWitt went over to Ellie and led her gently to the piano bench. He kept looking her straight in the eye, the way snake charmers are supposed to do. Ellie looked as if she might bolt at any minute, but she sat down.

I sighed. "I guess we could work in some stuff between the Great Penwiper and the head cheerleader."

"That's right. All we have to do is add another verse to the song," DeWitt said, smiling at Ellie.

I squinted at Ellie out of the corner of my eye. This getting-revenge stuff was taking a peculiar turn. How would the cools take to being mocked by the likes of

Ellie Siegel? Nobody could have looked less like a cool than Ellie. Ellie looked positively *anti*cool. Without meaning to, I started to laugh.

Ellie rolled her eyes toward me.

"It's not you, Ellie," I managed to blurt. "Or, rather, it *is* you. It's all of us. I just got an idea for the name of our group. The Anticools."

Ellie glanced at DeWitt uneasily. But he was raising his glass of limeade. "As Señorita Taylor would say, *perfecto*! A toast. To the Anticools!"

"To the Anticools!" I clinked my glass against his. I even allowed myself a grin at Ellie.

*

I'd noticed it before. The way time speeds up and slows down, depending on what you're doing. Now it was happening again. The time DeWitt and I spent rewriting the skit and teaching Ellie how to imitate girls like Veronica, that went very slowly. Every time Ellie did something clumsy, she'd threaten to quit the skit and burst into tears. I'd start to get mad, but DeWitt would step in and explain quietly how a good comic can turn clumsiness into laughs. He sounded so matter-of-fact about it that Ellie would always calm down. This only took about a week all in all, but it seemed more like a year.

Then tryouts and rehearsals started, and the days spun by as if DeWitt and Ellie and I were on a merry-go-round with the motor turned up to high.

Miss Pattrick loved the skit, of course. She said it was

"a clever satire." I couldn't wait to find out what the cools would do when they saw it. Hardly any of the big seventh-grade cools were in the show. Just a couple in the boys' octet. I had expected Veronica Allison to try out for sure, and as soon as Veronica got wind of what we were doing, it would be all over school. But Veronica was a cheerleader, and at this time of year all the cheerleaders were tied up at track meets.

Then I kept thinking one of the other kids at rehearsals would leak the news of our skit to David Lear and that David would suddenly rush on stage one afternoon foaming at the mouth. But only a few skits rehearsed at a time, and the eighth- and ninth-graders who rehearsed when we did either didn't know David or just didn't care what we were doing.

So much the better for our revenge. Come the night of the show, David and his friends would be in for a nasty surprise.

One afternoon DeWitt and Ellie and I were on the stage rehearsing. DeWitt was just finishing a verse:

> And anyone who doubts us is a fool,
> For we are the epitome of cool.

Ellie was supposed to bat her eyes like Veronica and slink around the stage while he sang. As the Great Penwiper, I was supposed to chase her, drooling. We were getting pretty good. Ellie slunk like she had arthritis, but that only made it funnier.

"Way to go, girl," DeWitt said. "You're going to make old Veronica Allison swallow her teeth."

Ellie stopped slinking and gave DeWitt a sudden big smile. I'd have sworn there were tears in her eyes. De-Witt smiled back and started the next verse.

That's when one of the back doors opened and three big old greasers came into the auditorium with Mickey Blake. They had to be ninth-graders at least, and they looked mean. Pale and fat and mean. Mickey trotted alongside them like a small dog they were walking.

The greasers started booing. "Hey, get off!" they shouted. "No nigs with white girls! No nigs on our stage!"

Ellie and I stopped dead. My heart pounded.

Mrs. Clauson lifted her hands from the piano in the middle of a transition. She cocked her head expectantly but did nothing more. Miss Pattrick had been huddled with the costume committee next to the stage door. Now she straightened her silk neck scarf and started walking slowly, very slowly, up the aisle toward Mickey and his friends. "Are you boys planning to be in this production? I don't seem to recognize you."

"Hey, lady. Hey, teach. No nigs!" one of the fat, pale greasers yelled.

Miss Pattrick kept walking. "I'm afraid I can't tolerate that kind of language in this auditorium," she said crisply.

"We don't want no trouble with you," the greaser tossed back. "We just want that coon out of the show."

Miss Pattrick pointed to the doors. "You'll have to leave."

For a minute I didn't know whether they'd listen to

her or whip out knives. I'd never actually seen a knife in school, but I knew some of the hoods were supposed to carry them.

But the greasers started backing up. "This is just a friendly warning!" one of them said. Then they turned around and left, with Mickey pattering after them importantly.

Miss Pattrick looked relieved. She might have been a little afraid of those guys herself. "Does anyone here know those boys?" she called. "I think we ought to tell Mr. Reilly that they've been here."

But nobody seemed to know the greasers' names. My guess was that they didn't even go to Emerson. Mickey could have picked them up anywhere.

Mrs. Clauson hardly gave us a minute to recover. She sounded a chord on the piano, and when she had our attention, she picked up the song exactly where she'd left off.

DeWitt chimed in with the next line. The two of them seemed to have the same attitude. Nothing had happened. The show would go on.

*

You'd think that after a scene like that, the Clausons would at least have been a little nervous about the act. If they were, they didn't show it. Mrs. Clauson turned out to have the same talent for going blank as DeWitt. You might wonder what she was thinking, but you knew you'd never find out.

Ellie and I, on the other hand, were nervous wrecks.

"What if the greasers start a rumble?" Ellie whispered to me frantically after one rehearsal. "What if they throw a stink bomb onstage the night of the show?"

She kept on asking me questions like that. I didn't know what to say. I didn't know what I'd do if somebody threw a stink bomb at us. I didn't even want to think about things like that. Finally I just said, "Oh, shut up, Ellie," which made her start to cry and me feel guilty. Ellie wouldn't talk to me for about a day afterward.

At home things were completely different.

Aunt Zona could hardly wait for the night of the show. True, she was still a little reluctant about my doing an act with the Clausons. But now that Ellie was in the skit, she said, she felt better. "Now it's more even," she told me. I didn't get it until she explained, "Two colored and two white." Aunt Zona wanted to be able to tell her bridge club that DeWitt and Mrs. Clauson were in my act, not the other way around.

But Aunt Zona had another reason for being enthusiastic about the Troubador Show. "Wouldn't that be the perfect place to sell my divinity?" she asked me. "People always like to eat at a show. Remember when we went to see that cute Mitzi Gaynor in *South Pacific*? I thought you had a hollow leg, Billy Lou. All that popcorn!"

I told Aunt Zona that the principal wouldn't let her sell divinity at the show.

"Not even in the lobby? Why, I'd call that a service to the school."

I told Aunt Zona that the front hall of Emerson Junior High couldn't exactly be called a lobby. People didn't just set up and start selling things there.

"Well, all right!" Aunt Zona said sharply. "I'll leave the divinity at home. But I don't see any reason why I can't pass out my handbills, just like I did at your friend's recital. I won't even come into the building, I'll just stand on the front steps until the show starts. Unless you think your principal would call the paddy wagon on me for that, too!"

There was no point in arguing with Aunt Zona when she got that put-out look on her face. I knew I'd have to think of some way to short-circuit her before the night of the show. I had enough to worry about with the greasers and Ellie Siegel about to mess up the act at any second. Having my aunt pass out handbills to all the cools and their parents before the performance would spoil my plan for sure. That would be much worse than watching her do it at DeWitt's recital. After all, this was serious. This was revenge.

The night of dress rehearsal, as I was getting ready for bed, I could hear Aunt Zona's *Ten O'Clock News* program on the TV in the living room. Austin Ferlin was giving the weather. I recognized his voice from my room because he also played Calvin Coffin, the ghoul who hosted the Friday-night creature movies.

Ferlin's ghoul voice was talking about high winds. There was a tornado watch in western Kansas, and some storms might be heading this way over the weekend. That gave me an idea. "See, Aunt Zona?" I called after she'd turned off the set and gone into the bathroom to cold-cream her face. "This would be a terrible weekend to pass out handbills. The wind would blow them all away."

"Lordy, Billy Lou. You don't think I'd stay outside passing out handbills in a tornado. Not after what happened to your cousin Thelma!"

Cousin Thelma had been living out in Ruskin Heights a couple of years ago when the big tornado hit. Her whole house had been flattened like matchsticks, but Cousin Thelma hadn't been hurt because she'd been across the street at a neighbor's at the time. The houses on that side of the street hadn't even been touched.

"Come to that, if there's a tornado, the show will be canceled anyhow. It won't matter what I do with my handbills."

I stuck out my tongue in frustration. Aunt Zona couldn't see me do that because she was still slathering on the cold cream in the bathroom. I stood at the foot of my bed and frowned out the window. I should have known Aunt Zona wouldn't be scared by weather. I'd have to think of another way to scotch the handbills.

The night sky was almost clear. There was only a faint sickly haze around the moon to hint that a storm might be on the way. Austin Ferlin had said that one tornado had been sighted over Hutchinson, Kansas, but that was a long way west of Kansas City.

As I climbed into bed, I tried to picture a tornado

coming down on Emerson Junior High School. That would certainly take care of the cools once and for all. I could see them, David Lear and Claudia Hardcastle and Veronica Allison and all the rest, flung into the air like so many human matchsticks, shooting away in a roar of wind, gone forever.

No. I turned out my light. I didn't want a tornado to blow the cools away. I wanted to enjoy the expressions on their faces after they saw DeWitt and Ellie and me do our skit. What DeWitt had said to Ellie was right. The cools would swallow their teeth.

· Chapter Fifteen ·

ON SATURDAY MORNING, the air was dense and damp. The sky was awash with dirty-gray clouds.

As I came into the kitchen for breakfast, Aunt Zona had the radio turned on to another weather report. "Partly cloudy today, chance of showers late this afternoon, clearing tonight." No mention of tornadoes.

I was still worried. I wanted everything perfect for my revenge.

Aunt Zona tried to cheer me up. Pouring Karo syrup on my french toast, she said, "Just leave it in the hands of the Lord, Billy Lou. Pray for good weather tonight, and I'll pray, too."

I didn't know about praying for weather. Aunt Zona and I might be praying for good weather, but some farmer's family out in Blue Springs might be praying for rain. Would the prayers just cancel each other out? Anyway, I sort of had the idea that God was partial to a big storm. Look at the Bible. Noah's flood. Job's whirlwind.

But as Aunt Zona said grace over the french toast, I squeezed my eyes shut and sent up my request.

Maybe it worked. All day long the clouds pouted glumly overhead but never opened up into an honest rainstorm. Then around suppertime they began to scatter, as if an invisible hand were tidying up the sky over Kansas City.

By the time DeWitt and I left for school, it was almost clear.

DeWitt and I had to leave an hour before Aunt Zona because we had to put on our costumes and makeup at school. Mrs. Clauson had told us she'd be along later. Since she'd be sitting offstage at the piano, she didn't have to wear anything special, just a good dress.

I wanted to leave early for another reason, too.

I'd decided how to stop Aunt Zona from passing out her handbills. I'd have to use the direct approach. Steal the handbills.

Well, it wasn't actually stealing, I reasoned as I lugged the huge cardboard box out of the house while Aunt Zona was upstairs in her room. Stealing was what David Lear and the other cools did. I was only borrowing. I'd take the handbills to school with me, keep the box in a safe place during the show, and then return it to Aunt Zona later when there was no one around for her to pass things out to. Aunt Zona would be furious, but after the show was over she could ground me for two weeks and I wouldn't even care.

DeWitt was waiting on the sidewalk. "Here," I grunted, and made him hold half the box.

DeWitt didn't take much to being a smuggler. "This

is ridiculous, Louis," he kept saying as we shuffled crab-wise up Prospect Avenue with the box. That was the only way the two of us could walk with all those handbills between us. "What do you expect to do with this junk when we get to school? You couldn't possibly get this box into the boys' dressing room."

True. The boys' dressing room was at the top of a long, narrow flight of stairs backstage. I couldn't keep the handbills there because: (1) One of the teachers would be sure to see them and ask what they were. (2) DeWitt and I would ruin our insides trying to get the box up that steep staircase. We'd end up like poor Freddie Buscaglia, who had to have two hernia operations in one year when he was ten years old. (3) The dressing room was so tiny that there was barely room for the actors and their costumes, much less several thousand handbills.

As we rounded the corner of Emerson Parkway and headed for the school, I hit on a solution. "How about leaving the box outside the stage door?" I said.

The stage door was at the side of the building toward the back. Right by the row of rusty metal barrels that held the collected school trash. There was nothing much else back there, which was why kids liked to sneak out that door now and then for a quick smoke. At night the area should be totally deserted. There wouldn't be anyone to pick up the trash again until Monday.

"What if it rains?" DeWitt said.

"It won't."

By going around the block we were able to approach the stage door from the back. So nobody saw DeWitt and me set the big cardboard box down behind one of the trash barrels. It looked fine there. Like any other part of the trash. Even if someone happened to walk out this door during the show, they'd never suspect there was something that didn't belong.

DeWitt wasn't convinced. "Keep this up and we'll both end up in the pen at Leavenworth," he told me.

The stage door turned out to be unlocked. We let ourselves in and hurried up to the boys' dressing room. As I'd expected, the little room was jammed with kids. The air was heavy with the smells of greasepaint and sweat.

As I put on my Great Penwiper suit and my makeup, my stomach kept giving these little trills. I was excited, yes. But not scared. This, finally, was it. My night of revenge. I wouldn't have to wait any longer to show the cools up. "Revenge is sweet, revenge is sweet," I chanted softly to myself as DeWitt and I dashed back down to the stage.

All the different acts were milling around. Even though most people were whispering instead of talking, it still seemed noisy.

DeWitt and I stood to one side to wait for Ellie to come out of the girls' dressing room. From somewhere in the shadows under the catwalk, I thought I heard someone mutter something. *Nig?* I wheeled around, but all I could see was a couple of stagehands. They didn't look like hoods. I licked my lips. DeWitt wasn't paying any attention. Should I mention what I'd heard?

On the other side of the stage, Mrs. Clauson was standing by the piano. She waved. DeWitt smiled and waved back.

No, don't say anything. Maybe it was your imagination.

Through the closed curtains, I could hear the people pouring into the auditorium. A thousand people. Two thousand people. All going to see the Anticools. See our revenge.

Ellie joined us in the wings, wearing her baggy cheerleader outfit. She looked peculiar, all white.

"You okay, Ellie?" I said.

She swallowed and gave me a glassy look.

Miss Pattrick appeared beside me. I could smell her sweet perfume swirling between us. "Break a leg, everybody," she whispered as the stagehands began to pull the black velvet curtains apart.

The Anticools were one of the last acts, so DeWitt, Ellie, and I had to stand backstage waiting a long time. We waited through a baton twirler. The girls' glee club. A magician with a live duck. An eighth-grader who sang like Elvis Presley. A couple of dippy-looking guys who recited "The Charge of the Light Brigade" in unison. When it was finally our turn to go on, I was afraid my leg had gone to sleep. I stamped it a couple of times to get the circulation going.

Mrs. Clauson played our introduction.

DeWitt and I started to walk onstage. Ellie didn't budge.

"Wake up, Ellie!" I waved a hand in front of her eyes.

Ellie didn't blink. She didn't speak. She didn't do anything.

"Oh, no. Oh, no. She's got stage fright. Ellie, snap out of it. You hear me, Ellie?"

Mrs. Clauson got to the end of the introduction. She stopped. When we didn't come onstage, she started over again from the beginning.

DeWitt was hovering over Ellie. "Pinch her cheeks," I hissed. "Slap her wrists. I'm warning you, Ellie Siegel, if you mess up my one chance to get even with the cools, you're dead."

DeWitt shushed me. He whispered something that must have been encouraging in Ellie's ear. A little color came back into her face. Slowly, she began to move. Ellie walked like ice cracking, but she walked.

We were on.

At first it was touch and go. DeWitt sang, and Ellie and I did our shtick. Ellie's gestures were stiff and half-hearted. I was afraid she might just stop short and dash offstage. Then the audience laughed at the Great Pen-wiper chasing the cheerleader around the stage, and Ellie perked up. She gave the audience a Veronica-Allison-style wink, but her eyelashes seemed to stick together afterward, so that she couldn't quite get her eye to stay open. She kept poking at the lids with her fingers. I wasn't sure whether Ellie was faking or whether her gunky mascara had glued itself together, but the audience laughed again.

I relaxed. The act was working.

Ellie got more and more excited. When she gave her cheerleader cheer, her arms whirled like little helicopter blades and she made high, knock-kneed leaps into the air. The crowd seemed to love her.

It was hard to tell who was the star, Ellie or DeWitt. DeWitt's voice sounded clearer and cleaner than ever tonight:

> "Oh, we are the epitome of cool.
> If you dissent, we promptly overrule.
> It's very clear that we are boss.
> We have the style, we have the gloss.
> We're never rude but we are often cruel,
> For we are the epitome of cool."

The last *cool* was a high note. DeWitt held it for a long time. The word *cool* sliced through the audience's loud applause and stirred the Missouri flag at the edge of the stage.

The audience started clapping again. When we took our bows, DeWitt got an extra-loud hand. And Ellie. She actually got a few whistles from the balcony.

Ellie lost her head and started blowing wet kisses at the audience. That was when we decided to get her off. DeWitt took one arm and I took the other, and while the audience still clapped away, we carted Ellie into the wings.

For the rest of the show the three of us stood by the light box, wiping sweat off our faces and hopping from one leg to the other. That is, I hopped. Because I knew the most important part of this night was coming after the last skit, when people started talking about the show.

What would the cools say?

I found out soon enough. The last skit was the boys' octet singing "The Lord's Prayer." Something like that was bound to be the last skit at a school show. Sometimes it was the school song instead, but it was always something serious.

As soon as the curtains closed, a whole mob of people from the audience began jamming into the wings and onto the stage. Most of them were parents, but a few kids mingled in.

The first seventh-graders I saw were Veronica Allison and David Lear. Paul was trailing along after them with some blond girl I didn't know.

I nudged Ellie and DeWitt and took a deep breath.

Anything could happen now. The cools could hit us. Pinch us. Bite us. Pass a law against us in student council. Never speak to us again. Bully the rest of the school into never speaking to us again. For all I knew, the Pendragon had a private line to the superintendent of schools, and after tonight, none of us would ever graduate.

It didn't matter. We were even.

"Louis!" Paul spotted me right off. He headed straight at me, pulling the girl along with him. "That skit!"

I stood my ground. Crossed my arms. Waited.

David jostled his way next to Paul. "Did you write all that yourself?"

"That's right." I jutted out my lower lip. Dared him to say more.

"Out-standing!" David said. "Congratulations, sport. I never knew you could be so hilarious. How'd you ever think of those dumb characters?"

"I didn't think that cheerleader part was so hilarious," Veronica said peevishly.

Was David kidding? "Wait a minute," I said to Paul and David. "Are you saying you liked the skit?"

"Of course we liked it!" Paul said. "You were a big hit, Louis. Everybody says so."

"Except that the cheerleader part would have been much cuter with a *real* cheerleader in it," Veronica said. She gave Ellie a withering look.

"Maybe you can write another skit for Veronica," David said, giving Veronica's shoulders a squeeze. "Maybe we can all be in the next one."

"But—"

Paul said into my ear, "By the way, I don't know if you're interested, but there's a big after-the-show party at the Goodpasters' tonight. Only don't bring those two." He pointed at DeWitt and Ellie. "See you later, maybe."

The cools were moving off into the crowd. "You're a riot, sport. I always did say you had real talent." David waved at me, grinning.

For a few seconds I felt a traitorous leap of excitement in my chest. *You're a riot, sport.* Louis Lamb, class clown, a real riot. At the top of the "Knite Life" column. But then I looked at DeWitt and Ellie, and I remembered. I didn't want David Lear's approval anymore. "All that work," I said finally. "All that work, and they aren't even mad. They don't even get the point."

"They said we were a hit," Ellie said mildly. "Didn't you want to be a hit, Louis?"

My fists clenched. "No, Ellie, I did not want to be a hit. I wanted to *get even.* You don't get it either, do you? If they liked it, we aren't even. Now we'll never be even!"

I shoved Ellie to one side and pushed my way through the crowd. I made my way to the back hallway and started down the stairs leading to the stage door. I had to get some air.

I heard footsteps behind me. "Louis, wait!" DeWitt called.

I kept on going.

"Louis!" DeWitt's hand closed on my shoulder. I had to stop to keep my balance. "Come on, Louis, wait up a second."

I was breathing heavily. Partly from dashing downstairs, partly from being mad. "It's so unfair!" I gasped. My breathing echoed around us in the deserted stairwell. "We can't even get a decent revenge on those people."

"Take it easy. You're getting yourself all upset, and it's not worth it. Believe me, it's not."

"What's the matter with you, anyway?" I shook his hand off. "Don't you have any feelings? Can't you see? The cools still have all the power. They can approve of us whether we want them to or not. It doesn't make a bit of difference what you do or I do or Ellie does. We're at their mercy forever and ever. Like us or not like us—we have no control over it. It's just not *fair!*"

"Ah." I couldn't tell if it was a sigh or a word. De-Witt gave me a sad smile. "Still worrying about *fair*. You poor sap. Haven't you figured it out *yet?*"

"Figured what out?"

DeWitt's smile got sadder and broader at the same time. "You said it a minute ago yourself. It's just not fair. Of course not. Life isn't supposed to be fair. Never was, never will be. You've got to get that through your head once and for all, Louis. Repeat after me. Life. Is. Not. Fair."

"But if that's true, how can you stand it? How can anybody stand it? God!" A featherlike chill ran down my spine. *God!* This was the first time I'd ever said that word that way. Like a curse word. If Aunt Zona could only hear me now. She'd flay me alive.

"My granddaddy's a minister. You know what he says?"

I shook my head and wiped my face with my fingers. Makeup came off on them.

"He says, 'God never explains nothing to nobody. All he ever gives you is enough to go ahead on.' "

We stood in the empty stairwell looking at each

other. I don't know how long we stood there. Minutes seemed to drop down from the top of the stairs and disappear into the shadows at the bottom by the stage door. My breathing slowed. All I knew was that I was beaten for good. No more getting even. How would I act toward the cools after this? I thought it over for a second. It didn't matter, I decided. It just didn't matter.

It was DeWitt who remembered first. "Say, as long as we're down here, what about your aunt's handbills?"

"Oh, Lord!" I slapped my forehead. "I forgot! On top of everything else, I've got to go back upstairs and face Aunt Zona with the handbills."

"Come on." DeWitt started down to the door ahead of me. "She probably won't be all that mad. She'll be thinking about what a big hit we were tonight, and she'll be so proud, she'll forgive you."

Maybe. I didn't have the strength to argue about Aunt Zona. At least DeWitt was willing to help me drag that monster box back up to where Aunt Zona would be waiting. I followed DeWitt down the rest of the stairs and out to the trash barrels.

The first thing I saw when we stepped outside was an orange dot. Then another orange dot, swinging through the night air next to it. And another. Three dots, three glowing orange trails in the dark. But no faces. Just the quiet glow of three cigarettes.

The stage door clicked shut behind us.

A voice said, "Well, lookee here at what just fell into our laps. One blue-eyed nig and one nig lover." My eyes were beginning to adjust. I could just make out a large shape in a leather jacket. "Saved us having to look you up. Ain't that convenient."

The voice was sickeningly familiar. It sounded like one of the fat greasers who had busted into our rehearsal with Mickey Blake. I turned back toward the door, but another leather-jacketed shape had moved between it and us.

"Hey, boy," the second shape said to DeWitt. "You're in trouble. You should have listened to the warnings when they were still friendly."

"Now, didn't we tell you?" said the third shape. "We don't want any nigs playing around with little white girls. Not in this neighborhood. You like to sing and dance? Then go on back down to Twelfth and Vine and do it."

I looked around, wild with the hope that I could think of something to stop what was going to happen. If we could kick the trash barrels over. Make a lot of noise. Almost everyone would be on the other side of the building, but maybe one or two strays would be close enough to hear.

Too late. The hoods were moving toward us on three sides. We were trapped.

DeWitt managed to yell at me. "Run—"

But they were on us. Two of the hoods stamped out their cigarettes and grabbed DeWitt. I was turning toward him when I felt the blow on my back. I caught my balance just as the guy behind me hit me a second time, on the neck.

The pain was so terrible that I doubled over on the ground. By the time I could pull myself partway up, they were leaving with DeWitt, half carrying, half dragging him. One of them had an arm over his mouth.

I saw them half a block away, just a jumble of shapes between two street lamps, lurching toward the park. Then the pain swept over me again, and when I got myself back up I couldn't see them anymore.

The park had swallowed them.

·Chapter Sixteen·

SLOWLY I OPENED my eyes. It was like waking up in a still, warm oven. Nothing stirred in my bedroom. The curtains hung limply against the window frame. As I turned my head slightly, I could see the tan paint on the wooden sill, beginning to chip with age.

"Aunt Zona?"

I struggled to sit up. The thudding pain in my back suddenly made me remember everything. It was Sunday morning. I was home in bed with a bruised neck and back, and DeWitt was in the hospital with his head and chest half beaten in, and it was all my fault.

"Aunt Zona?" I said again. Still no answer.

Carefully, carefully, I slid my feet off the bed and onto the floor, balancing myself against the bedpost. When I stood up, I wasn't sure I could take a step. I was dizzy. Stiff, too. I hadn't fallen asleep until after three in the morning. According to the clock on my bureau, it was almost nine now.

My stomach growled. Where could Aunt Zona be? On most Sundays she would have gotten me up half an hour ago and had a fancy pancake breakfast hot and waiting in the breakfast room.

Somehow I made it into the bathroom. I stood at the sink, splashing cold water on my face and into my dry, bitter mouth. I remembered everything, all right. Last night I'd finally stumbled back into the school and found Miss Pattrick and Mrs. Clauson and Aunt Zona, and they'd called the police. The sirens must have scared away the greasers, because the policemen never saw them.

The only person they found in Emerson Park was DeWitt. He was unconscious. They rushed him to the hospital, with Mrs. Clauson riding in the same ambulance. Aunt Zona and I followed behind in a squad car, and while a doctor in the emergency room checked to be sure I wasn't hurt badly, the police talked to me, taking down my vague descriptions of the hoods. I told them I didn't know the guys' names. The best lead I could give them was to talk to Mickey Blake. The police sounded disappointed, but they said they'd go over to Mickey's house later.

The doctors must have taken DeWitt to another room, because after we got to the hospital, I didn't see him. Later the police drove Aunt Zona and me home, and that was all.

I didn't know what had happened during the night. Had the police ever caught up with those hoods? I could still smell that disinfectant hospital smell. Was DeWitt all right? What was happening to him right now?

The cold water didn't make me feel much better, but it did wake me up. As I turned off the tap, I heard the screen door open in the living room.

"Aunt Zona?" I walked into the dining room, and there she was.

"How are you, punkin? Did you sleep at all?"

"I'm okay," I muttered. "Where have you been?"

Aunt Zona had started to touch my forehead, the way she did when she thought I might have a fever. My question seemed to make her pull back. Aunt Zona glanced up at the chandelier, as if another person in the room might be sitting on it. "Oh, I was next door. You want some breakfast, Billy Lou?"

I followed her to the kitchen. "You were next door? You mean you went to the Clausons' house?" I couldn't be hearing right.

"Well, yes." She still wasn't looking at me. "I took a little casserole over to Miz Clauson. I thought she wouldn't have much time for cooking with her boy in the hospital. Oh, Billy Lou!" Now our eyes met. Aunt Zona looked surprised—at what, I wasn't sure. "It's just a sin and a shame, what that poor woman's going through. She didn't get to bed all night. When I came over, she'd barely been home from the hospital five minutes. It's her only boy."

Even though the air was hot and close, my hands were like ice. "Did—did you talk about DeWitt? Did she say how he was? When can I see him?"

Aunt Zona got a box of corn flakes out of a cabinet and started shaking them into a bowl. "The doctors say he had a concussion, but he'll probably be all right. He regained consciousness early this morning, and that's a good sign. He has some broken ribs, too. He'll have to stay in the hospital a few days, till they're sure there won't be any complications. He can't have any visitors except family right now. But maybe you can call him in a day or two."

"He'll be all right, though? That's what they said?" I wanted to shake the answers out of Aunt Zona the way she was shaking the corn flakes out of the box.

"Probably. You know what Miz Clauson said to me?" Aunt Zona asked over her shoulder. "She said, 'DeWitt's a survivor. He'll be fine.' Said it real quiet and proud. 'DeWitt's a survivor.'" Aunt Zona set the bowl of cereal down on the breakfast table, shaking her head. "I just don't think I could hold up the way she does if something that serious happened to you. I don't know how she does it." She got some milk out of the refrigerator and doused the corn flakes with it. "What are you looking at me like that for, Billy Lou?"

I sat down in front of the corn flakes. "I don't know. I guess it's the idea of you going over to the Clausons' by yourself. It just doesn't seem like you."

"Doesn't seem like me to help a neighbor out when she has some hard luck?" Aunt Zona's eyes flashed. She sounded normal again. "Now, when have I ever not done the decent Christian thing for a neighbor? I hope to goodness you know me well enough by now to give me a little credit, Billy Lou."

I let it pass. There was no point in reminding Aunt

167

Zona of all the things she'd said about colored people. She'd just pretend she'd forgotten all that. Anyway, I had no right to criticize now. It was because of me that DeWitt had gotten beat up in the first place. "Aunt Zona," I said through a mouthful of corn flakes. "I'm really sorry about everything. I know I'm to blame."

Aunt Zona pulled out the chair next to me and sat down with a small bounce. "To blame? To blame for what?"

I tried to keep on chewing. It was the only way I could get this out, chew and talk at the same time. "DeWitt got attacked because he was helping me go after your handbills. The only reason those handbills were behind the trash in the first place is because I made DeWitt help me sneak them there. It was stealing, and it was stupid, and because of me, DeWitt could have got murdered by those hoods."

"Billy Lou Lamb, you wipe those thoughts clean out of your head. I never heard such foolishness. You didn't know those hoodlums were out there. And remember, they didn't just go after DeWitt. They went after you, too."

"But the handbills. That was *my* idea. I forced De-Witt into it."

Aunt Zona harrumphed. "I get the feeling that your friend DeWitt would be a hard one to force into doing anything he didn't want to do. And as for the hand-bills—well, I've had a little time to think this morning, Billy Lou. You know, your grades are good and you write so lovely and all. You probably won't have any trouble getting a scholarship to college. And this house has been good enough for me for nearly thirty years. I guess we can stick it out here a little longer. So all in all, I don't suppose I'll need to be selling my divinity to so many people. It doesn't matter about the handbills."

I stirred my corn flakes around and around, trying to take in what Aunt Zona had said. Maybe she was right. Maybe it wasn't all my fault about DeWitt. But no matter whose fault it was, DeWitt had gotten really hurt.

Just the thought of those hoods got me riled up all over again. I wished they were the ones who'd been driven away in an ambulance. I wished the police would find them and throw them in jail. I wished DeWitt and I could get even. But it might never happen. Maybe the police would get something out of Mickey Blake—but maybe not.

"What about church?" Aunt Zona was standing up again, brushing her dress off with her hand. "You think you can get ready in time?"

"Church!" A few corn flakes exploded out of my mouth with that single word. "I don't want to go to church! I may never go to church again as long as I live!"

And now I knew who I was really mad at. I was mad at the hoods, of course. Who wouldn't be? But there was someone else to blame. "How can I go to church and pray to God when all the time he lets terrible things happen to people who don't deserve it? He let those guys take DeWitt and pound him, even though DeWitt never did anything to them. He lets crooks like David Lear run everything at school and get all the credit for things they never did. You want me to believe in a God who does things like that?"

Aunt Zona stood there looking at me, not moving. After a moment, she nodded. "All right. If that's the way you feel, I'll go by myself this morning. I know you're upset right now. Later when you think about it, you'll be sorry for what you just said."

"I won't." I shook my head. "I won't be sorry."

Surprisingly, Aunt Zona didn't argue with me. But on her way out of the kitchen, she stopped at the door. "We'll talk about this later," she said. Then she was gone.

I stayed in the kitchen while Aunt Zona got ready for church. From the breakfast room window I could see the ugly dark sky outside. It looked as if we might get that storm after all. Even with the window open high, the kitchen was as hot and dead-feeling as my bedroom had been.

As long as I lived, I'd never understand Aunt Zona. Going over to the Clausons' with a casserole. Suddenly giving up on the handbills and the divinity. What on earth could have got into her? Could what happened to DeWitt have affected her that much?

After a while, I heard the screen door open and shut again. Aunt Zona was on her way.

I decided to get dressed and write in my journal. Mostly questions. I had a lot of things to think through. About DeWitt, about Aunt Zona. About the cools.

Why had I spent so much time trying to become one? Today I found I didn't know. I honestly didn't care very much about cools. I cared about DeWitt.

I couldn't get a T-shirt over my head. It hurt too much. So I pulled on some jeans and a short-sleeved shirt with the buttons all open. I got my journal and a pen out and took them into the dining room, where I hoped there might be a little more air than in my bedroom.

There wasn't much. With Aunt Zona gone, the house was quiet. It was a thick quiet. Kind of an *occupied* quiet, I thought as I sat writing, as if an enormous creature somewhere in the house was almost through holding its breath.

When the doorbell rang, I jumped. My pen skipped across the page, leaving a wavy trail of blue-black ink behind it.

"Who is it?" I called with a foolish squeak.

"It's me, Louis." I knew the voice. Ellie Siegel's.

I got up faster than I should have. My back throbbed angrily. I had to take it easy on my way to the door. "Good grief. Ellie, what are you doing here?" I opened the screen and let her in.

"I just brought this over for you to sign." Ellie thrust a white envelope at me. I opened it and pulled out a greeting card. "HOSPITALS ARE THE DOGGONDEST PLACES," it said. A droopy-looking spaniel in a nurse's uniform stood on the cover carrying a thermometer.

"It's for DeWitt," Ellie said. "I heard about what happened after you guys disappeared last night. I thought you'd like to have your name on the card, too."

"Oh. A card. Sure, Ellie, I'll sign it." My pen was still in my right hand. I started scrawling my name while Ellie stood by, waiting. "They say he's going to be all right," I told her, as cheerfully as I could manage.

"He'd better be," Ellie said. There was an odd edge to her voice. A tone I'd never heard before. "DeWitt Clauson is just about the only kid in that school who ever treated me like a real person. Except for you, Louis. Sometimes."

I hoped I wouldn't blush. Ellie made me feel guilty. *Sometimes* was right. I handed the card and the envelope back to her.

"I'm not surprised at what happened," Ellie said, still with that peculiar edge. "Someone as nice as DeWitt could never last long at Emerson Junior High. I knew they'd get him, sooner or later."

"They? You know those greasers?"

Ellie shrugged. "I don't have to know them. I know the school. I know how things work. Good people get stomped on. Well, I won't bother you any longer—I've got to go mail this. See you, Louis."

Ellie was out the door before I could think of the next thing to say. I watched her stiff back as she walked down the street toward the mailbox. Funny, I thought. Ellie had changed, too, just like Aunt Zona. But talking to the new Ellie made me shrink a little. The new Ellie was cold.

Ellie dropped her card into the mailbox, turned the corner, and disappeared.

I walked back to the dining room, dropped my pen on the table, and pulled a chair up to the dining room windows. Outside, swollen purplish-green clouds were marching across the morning sky. A storm was coming, all right, and it was going to be a whopper. Maybe Kansas City was going to have a tornado at last, just like the one that hit Ruskin Heights. I hoped Aunt Zona would get home from church before the storm began.

I kept thinking of the questions I'd been writing in my journal.

Why? Why did anything happen the way it did? Why the cools and the hoods and the park?

Why did DeWitt have to be lying banged up in some hospital bed while I sat by the windows with only a few bruises, wondering why?

Repeat after me, Louis. Life. Is. Not. Fair.

That's what DeWitt had said, and there was no denying it. I knew for sure now that life wasn't fair. And I knew for sure that I'd never understand why.

Aunt Zona would say that it was all the will of God. That for some mysterious reason God let everything happen the way it did because in the end good would come out of it. Could that be true? Aunt Zona was treating the Clausons differently now. That was good. But did DeWitt have to be bashed by thugs in order for that to happen?

I looked up at the clouds, half hoping an answer might be written there in sky writing.

DeWitt had said something else, though. That idea of his grandfather's. *God never explains nothing to no-*

body. All he ever gives you is enough to go ahead on.

Enough to go ahead on. Aunt Zona had that. She baked her casserole and forgot about her handbills and went on off to church, just like she did every Sunday. Mrs. Clauson had it. She stayed up all night with De-Witt and the next morning talked calmly to Aunt Zona about DeWitt's being a survivor. DeWitt had it. He'd had it from the very beginning, from that first day of school when Mickey Blake and his friends tripped him in the gym, and DeWitt got right back up again.

Did I have it, too?

I had my journal. It still lay on the dining room table, open to the half-finished page of questions where a wavy trail of ink marked the point when Ellie rang the doorbell. In a few minutes, I would get up and finish the page. Eventually I would finish the whole journal. I didn't know what I was going to say, but I knew I'd keep on writing.

And DeWitt. I had DeWitt. Before long I'd see DeWitt and we'd talk everything over, and I still wouldn't understand any of it, but we'd go on being friends, maybe better friends than ever.

And after that?

I didn't know what would happen after that. All I had was enough to go ahead on.

A tiny unexpected gust of wind blew across my chin.

I turned back to the window and watched while the storm clouds mounted in the sky like some dark army on its way to battle. I sat at the open window a while longer and listened for the rising wind.